KU-454-849

G?LD MEDAL MYSTERIES

THIEF ON THE TRACK

MULTI-MEDAL WINNING PARALYMPIAN

ELLIE ROBINSON

ILLUSTRATED BY JAMES LANCETT

SIMON AND SCHUSTER

CHAPTER 1
ON YOUR MARKS

The Tokyo National Sports Stadium was spectacular. As host to the twenty-fifth Games, it was by far the biggest sports arena that Hannah Walker had ever been to. It was so vibrant and colourful as all the flags of the world danced in the wind. Hannah could hardly hear her dad speak over the excitement of the crowd. She watched a group of school children waving the Japanese flag as they saw themselves on the big screen. In the front row, Hannah brushed bits of popcorn off of her navy jumpsuit. Her dad rolled his eyes and laughed.

'You don't want to get food down that! You've been planning that outfit all week!'

'I'm just glad it's not ketchup.' Hannah rummaged through the maps and notebooks inside her satchel and looked up at her dad. 'Do we have our flag?'

He unfurled a Union Jack from his pocket. 'Of course we do!'

'Can I hold it?' asked Hannah. 'It might get us on the big screen!'

Her dad grinned. 'We're in the front row. I'll hang it over the railing for you!'

He held out the flag in the wind and attached it at either end of the railings.

Before Hannah could thank him, the lights in the stadium went out and music blasted from the speakers. The moment had finally arrived. The final of the men's one-hundred-metre sprint.

Over her shoulder Hannah heard an American voice squeak, 'Look! The one-hundred-metre dash!' Hannah smiled. She'd never heard that name for the race. It made her feel even further from her home in London, but in a good way. Everybody in the stands went wild as the big screen lit up and the tannoy announced, *Ladies and gentlemen! Please welcome your athletes for the men's one-hundred-metre final!*

Hannah leaned over the barrier to catch a glimpse of the emerging sprinters. All she could see was a spotlight shining at the end of the athlete tunnel. The crowd fell silent in anticipation. Hannah's dad grinned and whispered into her ear, 'Here they come!'

All of a sudden, a beam of light illuminated the track. A name appeared on the screen and the loudspeaker announced, *'In lane eight... Christoph Leichum of Germany!'*

Christoph emerged from the tunnel and waved to a cluster of people in Team Germany T-shirts. The spectators settled down when the next lane lit up and the announcer declared, *'In lane one... Lance Clark of the United States of America!'* There was a particularly big cheer from the American fans. Hannah watched the athletes already on the track stretching as the loudspeakers blared, *'In lane seven... Arturo Maggio of Italy!'* Maggio ran out from the tunnel and leaped into the air.

'In lane two... Jayden Francis of Jamaica!'

The big screen at the end of the stadium caught Hannah's eye. It showed a group of Jamaicans in the crowd, jumping up and down, with the flag of black-and-green triangles with yellow stripes painted on either cheek.

'In lane six—' Hannah pulled out her special competition programme from her satchel as the next name was called out – *'Nathan Henrie of Canada!'*

She flicked through the handbook to find the 'Start-Line Star Stats': a fact file about the athletes. As Hugh van Luben walked out to lane three to a wave of cheers from the Dutch, she landed on the box she'd been looking for: *Marks vs Tanaka – the two biggest rivals in all of sporting history*. With one gold medal each from the last two Games, this was the deciding race. The entire stadium had fallen silent as the announcer built up the tension. In the darkness, lane five was lit up in gold and Haru Tanaka's name was plastered across the boards in the stadium.

The tannoy boomed, '*In lane five, representing Japan...*' Everybody held their breath. '*Gold medallist and world-record holder... HARU TANAKA!*'

The stadium erupted with a level of noise Hannah had never experienced before. As Tanaka walked out to his adoring fans, she and her dad let out a cheer. The Japanese superstar took his place behind the starting blocks and waited as the final name was called out. The only name that had a chance of beating Tanaka. Now lane four went up in lights. This time in red, white and blue. Hannah got up from her seat to catch a glimpse of the final athlete as he emerged from the tunnel.

'*In lane four... representing the United States of*

America . . .' The athlete raised his hand in the air. 'Jesse Marks!'

After the cheers for Tanaka, Hannah didn't think the stadium could get any louder. Yet, as the American hero walked out on to the track, the atmosphere was electric – a rush of cheers and stomping. It was impossible to tell one nation's fans from another's as everybody got to their feet to applaud Jesse. Hannah watched as the American peeled back one side of his headphones to listen to the noise.

Chants of 'Jesse! Jesse!' rang out for everybody to hear.

Jesse kept his head down and raised his arm into the air. He gave a little wave to the crowd, before arriving behind his starting block and dropping his kit into a plastic box.

With all the runners now making their final preparations, the chants for Jesse were still ringing out. Hannah beat her hand on the railings to the rhythm. 'Jesse! Jesse!'

A smart official stood at the side of the track in grey trousers and a navy blazer. *She must be the starting official*, thought Hannah. The woman raised her hand and each of the sprinters made their way to the blocks. The Games volunteers put their fingers to their lips and the big screens displayed QUIET PLEASE. Within seconds the crowd fell silent and Hannah's chest went tight with suspense. The official with the starting gun stood up and brought what looked like a walkie-talkie to her mouth.

'*On your marks . . .*' said a speaker from each of the blocks.

The athletes took their start positions and Haru stamped his foot against the wedge. The clatter echoed around the stadium.

'*Set.*'

Hannah was almost hanging over the railings now. The sprinters were coiled and ready to strike.

BANG!

At the sound of the gun, the athletes launched themselves off the blocks and into the race. The crowd screamed as the Japanese athlete pulled out a tremendous lead with his world-famous lightning-fast start. Behind him came Marks, Francis and Maggio, all in a line. Hannah gasped and it seemed like the rest of the crowd gasped with her. Jesse had stepped up a gear and was powering down the second fifty metres. Desperate cheers from the spectators made Tanaka and Marks run even faster. Hannah saw the determination in Jesse's face as he refused to give up.

She found herself willing the American on. 'Go, Jesse!' she shouted.

The American closed the gap even further and with fifteen metres to go, the rivals were neck and neck. Hannah's dad joined her in yelling, 'Come on, Jesse!'

Hannah didn't dare blink. As Tanaka and Marks battled their way to the finish, the American appeared to have a toe in front! They stretched their necks in a last-ditch effort and dipped over the finish line. Everyone in the Tokyo National Sports Stadium looked up at the scoreboard in hope. Hannah leaped on to her chair when she saw the results. Jesse had won by two milliseconds! In a new world-record time!

'He's done it!' Hannah cried. 'He's won!'

She watched Haru crouched down on the track, gasping for air. He caught a glimpse of Jesse and shot to his feet to give him a hug. The smile on Haru's face lit up the big screen and his fans all jumped up to applaud him.

'Look!' Her dad pointed to the athletes on their lap of honour. 'They're coming this way!'

Hannah dived back into her satchel and pulled out her new compact camera.

'This is going to be my best photo yet!'

Not far away, she heard the clicking of big professional cameras. She leaned over the barrier to see Jesse and Haru posing together for the press. Hannah brought her camera to her face and pretended to be an international photographer herself, but she couldn't get a good shot.

'Ah, they're just too far away . . .' She sighed.

Hannah heard a young voice call out behind her.

'Hey, Jesse! Over here!' the girl shouted in an American accent.

Before Hannah could turn around, a girl who looked about her age, with glasses and long brown plaits clambered down on to the seat next to her and waved her arms in the air. 'Jesse!'

Hannah saw Jesse trying to follow the sound.

The girls took one look at each other, nodded and yelled as loud as they could.

'Jesse, over here!'

Jesse spotted the girls and led Haru over.

'They're coming!' Hannah beamed. 'It worked!'

Haru gifted Hannah a smile and posed with his Japanese flag. As she snapped away on her camera, the girl beside her pulled an American flag from her pocket and handed it to her hero.

'Thank you . . .' Jesse grinned. 'What's your name?'

Hannah felt everybody in the stand crowding around them as the girl replied, 'Maria.'

Jesse wrapped the flag around his shoulders like a cape.

'Thank you very much, Maria!'

Haru linked his arm through Jesse's as they both wore their flags like superheroes.

'Haru!' someone shouted down from the stands. 'Aren't you angry with Jesse for winning?'

The two athletes laughed.

'Of course not!' replied Haru. 'We're rivals for nine seconds, and friends the rest of the time.'

'I don't suppose that you have time for a quick photo with my daughter, do you?' Hannah's dad asked, taking her camera.

Hannah wasn't sure her beam could get any wider as both Jesse and Haru climbed up to the barrier and stood either side of her to pose. As her dad clicked, Hannah saw a woman with golden-brown curls in a long silk dress step over the row of seats.

'Quick, Maria!' She was gesturing to the American girl. 'Move in!'

'Mom . . .' The girl sighed, shuffling into the shot.

Hannah's dad chuckled. 'Smile, everyone!'

He and Maria's mum clicked their cameras and then thanked the two legends. Jesse high-fived the girls and turned back to the track.

'Thanks for the flag!'

Haru bowed to the crowd and rushed to rejoin his friend on their lap of honour. Hannah stared at her palm in awe.

'Wow!' She turned to her dad. 'I'm never washing my hand ever again!'

Maria squealed, 'Damn, I just met Jesse Marks!'

Her mum stashed her phone away and teased, 'I know you don't like photos, but I bet you're glad you've got that picture, aren't you?' She turned to Hannah's dad and smiled. 'Thank you for letting Maria join the photo.'

'Being together is what these Games are all about!' He beamed. 'And Hannah doesn't mind – do you, Hannah?'

Hannah shook her head.

'Well, thank you, Hannah,' the lady said. 'I'm Carmella, by the way.'

'Nice to meet you.' Hannah's dad smiled. 'I'm Michael Walker.'

The adults began chatting and Hannah took her seat next to the girl.

'So you might have guessed, I'm Hannah.'

'I'm Maria.' The girl stuck out her hand.

Instead of shaking it, Hannah laughed.

'Oh.' Maria looked panicked. 'Do you not shake hands in England?'

'No, we do!' said Hannah. 'I just only have one arm.' She showed Maria the empty right sleeve of her blouse.

'Oh, in that case –' Maria cheerfully swapped hands – 'I'll offer you this one.'

The two girls shared a grin as they shook left hands.

'It's very nice to meet you, Maria,' Hannah replied.

CHAPTER 2
LUCKY SOCKS

'It's nice to meet you too,' said Maria. 'I never would have met Jesse without you!' She beamed. 'It's been my dream for ages!'

'So you're a big sports fan?' Hannah asked.

Over a stadium announcement, Maria laughed.

'You could say that.' She showed Hannah the special pass hanging around her neck. 'I'm a long jumper. I won a competition back home and my prize was a trip to the Tokyo Games.'

'That's so cool! You must know everything about the Games!'

'Well... the competition wasn't a quiz.' Maria chuckled. 'I won the prize for jumping the furthest.'

Hannah shook her head. 'Of course you did, sorry!'

Maria smiled. 'Well, you're kinda not wrong. I do

know a crazy amount about the Games.'

The crowd fell silent around them. Hannah's dad tapped her on the shoulder. 'Look! The medal ceremony for the women's long jump!'

Hannah and Maria peered over the barrier just as the tannoy blared, *'The winner of the gold medal... representing Germany... Katja Schultz!'*

Hannah and Maria watched with wide eyes as Schultz leaped on to the podium with her hands in the air. Amongst all the cheering, Hannah could hear an English voice from someone she guessed was around eleven years old too. She spun round and saw, a couple of rows behind her, a boy brandishing a German flag. A man she assumed was his dad placed a hand on the boy's shoulder as the national anthem began to play; Hannah quickly stood and faced the podium while she hummed along. She knew the anthem well from her love of Formula 1. One of the best drivers was German and they played the 'Deutschlandlied' every time he won. Hannah always joined in during the last part, when she remembered the words.

'Blühe, Deutsches Vaterland!'

The crowd gave Schultz a big round of applause as they all sat down.

The boy stretched over the rows of seats and said, 'You know the words too!'

Hannah turned and smiled. 'Yes, I know them from F1.'

The boy sat down on the row behind and tied his flag to his backpack.

'Ah, epic! My dad is German, so that's how I know them.'

Hannah looked around and asked, 'Is your mum here too?'

The boy shook his head.

'No, my parents aren't together any more. My mum lives in the UK and my dad is a German sports reporter . . . That's why we're here.'

'Ooh!' Hannah said. 'I wondered why you had a British accent.'

'I speak German too,' he said proudly.

'That's cool! I can't really speak any other languages.' Hannah turned to Maria beside her. 'Can you?'

Maria smiled. 'I actually speak Portuguese.' She pointed to her stylish mother, who had sunglasses perched on her head. 'My mom's from Brazil.'

'Do you live in Brazil?' asked the boy.

Maria nodded. 'We just moved out to Rio from the States.' She pointed again. 'You see the man sat next to her with dark hair? That's my dad.'

Hannah looked up at the Yankees basketball cap on his head. 'He's not from Brazil, is he?'

'Nah, he's American.' She chuckled. 'What gave it away?'

The three of them waved at Maria's dad. On his knee was a girl a few years younger than Maria.

'Is that your sister?' Hannah asked.

Maria sighed. 'Yeah. She's kinda annoying, but I love her.'

'She looks like you,' said the boy.

'Yeah, we have our mom's hair.' Maria pushed her neatly tied plaits over her shoulder. 'Thick and very curly.'

The ceremony music started up again and another group of athletes lined up to receive medals.

Hannah's dad turned to her with a grin.

'The one-hundred-metre finalists!' He took a look at the boy sitting behind them and laughed. 'Each time I turn around, you've got another friend!'

'I know, right? Dad, this is . . .' Hannah hesitated for a moment. 'Actually, I don't know.'

'Sebastian,' the boy answered. 'But everybody calls me Seb.'

'So we have Maria and Seb!' Hannah's dad brought his fingers to his chin in thought. 'I tell you what . . .' He pointed to Seb's and Maria's parents, who were chatting. 'Are those your families?' The two of them nodded. He stood up and patted his chair. 'Here, Seb. You take my seat and I'll go and join the adults.'

As Hannah's dad left, Seb clambered over the row and plonked himself down next to Hannah.

To the other side of her, Maria squeaked, 'I can see Jesse!'

The three of them pressed themselves up to the barrier, watching the podium.

'He's wearing his lucky socks!' said Maria, pushing up her glasses.

Hannah squinted. 'How in the world can you see that?'

Maria laughed and pointed to the screen. 'Because the camera is zooming in on them.'

'Hey.' Seb tapped Hannah on the shoulder. 'You're missing the presentation!'

Hannah took in the crowd's cheers as Arturo Maggio of Italy stepped forward to receive his bronze medal. He blew a kiss to the cluster of Italian fans to show his gratitude. Slowly the cheers died down in anticipation of the Japanese superstar up next.

'The winner of the silver medal... representing Japan...' Seb called out in time with the announcer.

Hannah joined in. 'Haru Tanaka!'

The appreciation for Haru inside the national stadium was enormous. A sea of white flags with red circles waved across the stands. Parents lifted children on to their shoulders to get a better view of the athlete. A group of security guards even had to chase an over-excited fan off the track.

Hannah looked up at the screen to see the biggest smile spread across Haru's face. As he was presented with his silver medal, he curled his fingers into the shape of a heart and held it up to the cameraman.

Hannah smiled. 'He really is happy.'

After letting out a whoop, Seb replied, 'It's epic. He doesn't need medals when he has the love of his fans!'

Hannah had never seen someone be so happy with second place. She took out her camera to capture the elation on Haru's face, and as the shutter clicked, she smiled. 'They don't love his medals. They love him.'

The speakers began to announce the winner of the gold medal and Seb quickly pointed to the American. 'Here we go!'

Hannah watched Haru applaud his rival. 'They're so—'

The crowd erupted before the announcer had even finished, cutting Hannah off. She shouted over the noise.

'They're both so kind to each other!'

Hannah couldn't hear a word of the tannoy over the volume of the spectators, especially Maria's dad, who was bellowing behind them.

Jesse sprang on to the top step of the podium, grinning wildly.

'You know, my dad says that medals bring you recognition,' Seb said, 'but personality makes you memorable.'

Jesse bowed before the prize-giver and allowed her

to drape the medal around his neck. Hannah gave her loudest cheer as Jesse beckoned Haru on to the top step. The pair squeezed together, arm in arm, and the crowd roared. All across the stadium, fans, volunteers and officials linked arms with one another. On the big screen, Hannah saw Jesse mouth to Arturo, *'Get up here!'*

Arturo carefully balanced himself alongside the other two, who bunched together to make room.

'This,' said Seb, 'is the most epic event I have ever been to!'

Maria turned to face him. 'Does your dad bring you to a lot of competitions?'

'The ones in the school holidays, yes.'

'Are you back here tomorrow?' Hannah asked.

He quickly shook his head but didn't explain why as the American anthem started up.

Standing up straight, Hannah and her friends turned to the flagpole and the US flag was hoisted into the air. She noticed how both Jesse and Maria brought their right hands to their hearts – and so many of the audience did too. There had to be thousands of Americans here, thought Hannah, but fans from all countries were cheering. Even the Japanese fans of Haru gave a huge round of applause at the end of the anthem's final note.

Hannah had never seen so many countries cheer together. She called out to her dad, passed him her camera and got Maria's and Seb's attention.

'Can we take a photo for my mum? She'll think it's so cool that we're together!'

'Why's that?' Seb asked as he grinned at the camera.

'Mum's a foreign diplomat, so her job is to help bring people together,' Hannah explained. 'She has this running joke that all nations do is argue, but this stadium is proof that they don't.'

'Wow . . .' said Seb. 'That job sounds serious!'

Maria looked a little confused. 'What's a diplomat?'

Hannah always loved explaining her mum's work.

'She basically goes around the world, talking to important people from every country.'

Seb laughed. 'Yep, that's very serious!'

'Do you want to do that?' Maria asked Hannah. 'When you're older?'

'Absolutely!' Hannah replied.

As the noise inside the stadium settled down and spectators began to file out, Hannah shuffled closer to her new friends. She told Seb, 'Maria's going to be a professional long jumper!'

'Really?' He turned to Maria and joked, 'Mention me

when you win a medal!'

'Me too!' said Hannah.

Maria smiled. 'Of course I will.'

Hannah looked at Seb.

'What?' He looked panicked.

She rolled her eyes and laughed. 'What do *you* want to do?'

He visibly relaxed. 'Oh, phew! I wondered why you were staring at me! I'm going to be an actor,' he told her proudly.

Before he could elaborate, his dad shouted from the seats behind them, 'Sebastian, are you ready?'

Seb shrugged and sighed. 'Yeah . . .' He faced the girls. 'It was nice to meet you both.'

Hannah frowned. 'You're definitely not coming back here tomorrow, are you?'

'Ah no, I'm not.' He shook his head. 'My dad's got interviews in the morning and then he's taking me to the media centre.'

'Oh, okay,' Hannah said.

'But if you're free in the morning,' Maria said, 'we could all go for breakfast?'

Hannah wasn't sure why she hadn't thought of that. They turned to the adults with big cheesy grins.

'Can I, Dad?' begged Seb. 'Please?'

'What's this?' said his father, smiling.

'Have breakfast tomorrow with Hannah and Maria!'

'If that's okay with their parents.' He turned to their families. 'Is that all right with you?'

Hannah's dad nodded. 'Absolutely! I'm meeting some colleagues at the Tokyo Skytree tomorrow morning, so Sebastian and Maria could come along and keep Hannah company?'

Maria's mum brought her hands together. 'That's a lovely idea!'

'We can take Isabella to the Sportpark to meet the mascot,' Maria's dad said. 'She's been begging to go and I know Maria isn't interested. She's too grown up for mascots!'

Seb turned to his dad. 'So I can go?'

'Yes, and in fact, I think I'll come with you.'

'Ugh, Dad!'

Seb's dad rolled his eyes. 'Not to annoy you! I'm interviewing the captain of the German hockey team and the Skytree would make the perfect setting.'

Hannah grinned. 'Amazing. Tomorrow, we're having breakfast at the Skytree!'

CHAPTER 3
BUSTER THE COLLIE

From inside the Skytree cafe on Floor 340, the view of Tokyo was phenomenal. Hannah felt her ears adjust with a pop to the pressure of being so high up. She bit her nails as she gazed out of the window to look down on the world, noticing how each tiny person, car and animal were all intertwined. She imagined a dog on the loose running down the street and being caught by a customer leaving a nearby shop. Then the owner running after the dog, causing a taxi to slam on its brakes as they crossed the road. Hannah opened her notebook to jot down a cool thought.

We are all characters in one big story – life.

As Hannah clicked her pen shut, a waitress with short black hair and a sweet smile came to the table and set down a variety of drinks.

'That's a super cute outfit!' She pointed to Hannah's white shirt and dark brown trousers. 'You look like a retro movie star!'

Hannah blushed. 'Thank you. I'm glad you like it.'

The waitress bowed and turned to the drinks on the table. 'Your dad ordered these for you and your friends.'

Hannah took a look at them, each in a tall, thin glass and a different bright colour.

'What are they?' she asked.

The waitress pointed to the lime-green drink. 'This is a melon cream soda.'

'Cream?' Hannah wasn't sure about that and melon together.

'Ice cream!' the waitress replied.

That sounded better! Hannah stole a glance at her dad. 'Cool, ice cream for breakfast!'

The waitress giggled.

'Would you like to know about the other drinks?'

She pulled her eyes away from the melon cream soda and nodded.

'The orangey-yellow one is a tropical gradient soda and the pink one is a pink lemon drink. That one is my favourite,' the waitress confessed. 'They use lemon sorbet and pink lemonade to make it!'

All three drinks were a treat she'd never be allowed at home, but Hannah had her eyes on one in particular. She thanked the waitress and slowly nudged the melon cream soda closer to her side of the table. Just as her fingers left the glass she heard a loud, 'Hey!'

Quickly pushing the glass back, Hannah looked up and saw Seb walking towards her in an effortlessly cool outfit: pastel striped shorts, a white T-shirt and a light pink shirt.

He waved and called out, 'This is pretty epic!'

Hannah sat up straight and waved back. 'You made it!'

He shrugged. 'Why wouldn't I?'

She shrugged too. 'I was worried that you and Maria would forget.'

'Forget to visit the tallest building in the world?'

'Tallest *tower*,' Hannah teased.

Seb smiled. 'The tallest *something*.'

He took a seat opposite Hannah and waved goodbye to his dad. Hannah watched Seb's dad and a camera crew pile into the lift.

'Where's he going?'

'To the Tembo Deck above us.' Seb pointed to the ceiling. 'You get an even better view of the whole city from there.' Before Hannah could ask anything else, he picked up the tropical gradient soda and examined the glass. 'Wow! What's this?'

Hannah smiled. 'Taste it and find out.'

Seb took a slurp from the straw and his eyes widened. 'I know what this is!'

'Really?' Hannah said, surprised. Had he been here before?

'Yes. It's mine.' He took another sip and looked up. 'You know . . . unless you want it.'

Hannah noticed a girl in the distance. She was dressed in patchwork shorts and a baseball jersey that Hannah thought she recognized.

'Is that Maria?'

Seb spun round and squinted. 'I think so.'

'Maria!' Hannah shouted. The girl turned around and smiled. 'Over here!'

Maria quickly headed towards the table and took a seat next to Seb.

'I think everyone in the cafe now knows that my name is Maria,' she mumbled.

'Perfect!' said Seb. 'No need to introduce yourself.'

'But they stared at me . . .'

'Who cares? I love being in the spotlight. You have to if you're going to be an actor!'

Maria pushed her glasses up her nose. 'Well, there's

only one person in the spotlight today.'

Hannah leaned closer. 'Who?'

'You don't know?' said Maria.

'No!'

Her eyes widened. 'You haven't seen the news?'

'What news?'

'Jeez, really?'

Hannah rolled her eyes. 'What news, Maria?!'

Maria pointed to a TV in the corner of the cafe. 'That news!'

In bold letters across the bottom of the screen, the headline read, MARKS' MEDAL STOLEN. A video was playing that showed Jesse talking to the media.

'Is that true? Jesse's medal has been stolen?!' Hannah asked, amazed.

'It's gotta be! It's all over the news,' said Seb.

'Why would someone do that?' Hannah scoffed. 'Money, I guess,' she added.

Seb suppressed a laugh. 'You think they're holding it ransom in a dungeon?'

'But what if it's true?' said Maria. 'Not the dungeon part, of course, but Jesse does have a lot of sponsorship deals. A thief could demand he pays them millions for his medal back!'

'That would be really cruel,' said Hannah. 'Jesse worked so hard for that medal.' She thought back to her taxi journey that morning. 'The radio in our cab ride here did keep mentioning Jesse's name, but it was all in Japanese and I just thought they were talking about the race.'

'Dad mentioned it to me this morning,' Seb said, shrugging. 'Is it really that big of a deal?'

'It's terrible!' Maria said. 'Poor Jesse. He must feel awful!'

She reached towards the melon cream soda as she continued talking. 'The police have no idea how it disappeared.'

Seb laughed. 'Well, if they can't find who did it, then maybe we should!'

Maria sipped the drink and immediately stuck out her tongue. 'Damn, that's sweet!'

Hannah grinned. 'I'll have that one, if you like!' she suggested quickly.

Maria nodded and picked up the pink lemon drink instead. 'I know you were joking, Seb, but we *could* try to find the medal. It would be such a great thing to do for Jesse!'

The three of them shifted their gazes from one to the other. Hannah thought about it. Finding the medal would be a pretty cool thing to do. But . . . if the police were stuck, what hope did they have?

But Seb was grinning. 'Yeah, why not! Let's do it! Let's find that medal!'

Hannah swallowed her doubt. 'Let's give it a go!'

Maria beamed. 'So, where do we start?'

Hannah delved into her satchel and pulled out a pen, her notebook and a map of the Sportpark. 'We need to make some notes,' she explained.

As she took hold of the pen, Seb blurted, 'Epic, you're left-handed like me!'

Looking at her one arm, Hannah smiled. 'Hmm, I suppose I am.'

Seb held his hand out for a fist bump. 'Us lefties have to stick together.'

'Hey!' said Maria.

He winked at her. 'I'm only teasing.'

'Oi! We can't fall out now.' Hannah said, straightening

out her fold-out map. 'We could start by connecting all the places where the medal has been?'

She clicked the top of the pen, ready to write.

'Right now, the police say they don't know when or where it went missing,' Maria said. 'So I guess we've just gotta list all the places it could have been?'

'The athletes' village?' Seb suggested.

'And the stadium,' said Maria.

Hannah circled their locations on the map. 'You're right, but they're both so big.' She tapped the paper. 'The stadium must have so many rooms behind the scenes.'

'And a warm-up area for the athletes,' added Maria.

'Yes, and they have a prep area too . . .' Moving her pen to the athletes' village, Hannah shook her head. 'The village is even worse. There are twenty-one apartment buildings, a food hall, a games room, an anti-doping building, casual-dining cafes, a gift shop, a plaza and a bus station.'

Seb looked impressed. 'Wow, how do you know all this?'

'It was a long flight over here and I like to read,' Hannah confessed.

She turned to her notebook and began biting her fingernails.

Maria frowned. 'What's wrong?'

'Nothing...' Hannah forced her hand away from her mouth.

'You sure?'

Hannah sank into her seat. 'This is already so difficult,' she admitted.

Seb pointed to the TV with a shrug. 'It was difficult for Jesse to win the medal, but he did it!'

'We could at least give it a try,' said Maria. 'Do it for Jesse!'

Seb held out his arms. 'Totally! What could possibly go wrong?'

Hannah fiddled with her pen. 'Don't you think this is a job for a detective?' she said as she watched Maria slowly stir her ice cream with a straw.

Maria let go of the straw. 'But there's a thirty-thousand-dollar reward.'

Seb's eyes lit up. 'Wow! Why didn't you tell us that?'

Maria pushed up her glasses. 'It's more about helping Jesse, isn't it? But actually, my family could really do with the money. My dad's gotta find a new job now that we're in Rio, and my mum spends all she earns on sending me to a good athletics club.'

Hannah felt a wave of guilt. 'Oh, I'm so sorry...'

'Don't feel sorry for me!' Maria said with a smile.

'Help me win ten thousand dollars!'

'Ten?' said Seb.

She rolled her eyes. 'Thirty divided by three is ten, isn't it?'

The other two grinned.

'Imagine what we could do with ten thousand dollars!' Hannah said.

Seb's hand shot up. 'I'd buy a dog!'

'That's one expensive dog,' Maria giggled.

Seb smiled. 'Buster needs food, toys, pet insurance, a bed...'

Hannah laughed. 'Buster?'

'Yeah! Buster the collie.'

'Aw, he already has a name!'

'What about you, Hannah?' said Seb.

'What would I spend ten thousand dollars on?' She pondered, but only for a second. 'All-access Grand Prix tickets!'

'Well, there we are. Three reasons to find this medal.'

Maria took a slurp of her drink. 'So let's work out where Jesse went after the ceremony, because wherever Jesse went, the medal went too.'

'Is there a way of seeing what the athletes are doing?' asked Seb.

'Like a diary?' Hannah suggested.

Maria frowned. 'I wonder if he keeps a diary. But even if he did, I'm not sure we'd be able to get hold of it.'

'Ooh!' Hannah could almost see the lightbulb ping above Seb's head. 'Social media! There's the Tokyo Games Social app where you can see posts from anyone involved.'

'Oh yeah, I've heard about that, but I don't have a phone,' Maria said sadly.

'I'll look!' said Hannah. She typed Jesse's name into the app and shook her head. 'Oh, Jesse doesn't have an account.'

'What? Not at all?' said Maria.

'Nope,' said Seb, who was looking at his phone too. 'So much for that idea!'

Hannah buried her phone into her pocket. 'Looks like we're going to do things the old-fashioned way, Holmes and Watson style.'

Maria nodded. 'It's gotta be better than nothing.'

Seb leaned forward. 'Who? What are you talking about?'

The girls raised their eyebrows at him.

'You know, Sherlock Holmes and Dr Watson...?' Maria prompted.

'Dr John Watson?' Hannah added.

Seb's face remained completely blank.

'Seriously?' said Maria. 'That doesn't ring a bell?'

Seb gave an awkward smile. 'Not really . . .'

Hannah's stomach growled and she looked about for the waitress. Behind her, she could hear Maria asking Seb, 'I thought you wanted to be an actor.'

'I do! But I've never done this play . . .' He fell quiet. 'Not a play? Hmm, book? Film? Opera?'

As the waitress came over to the table, Hannah turned back to Seb. 'We have a lot to teach you!'

The waitress opened up her flipbook and smiled. 'Is everything okay?'

Hannah smiled. 'Yes, thanks! Can we order some breakfast, please?'

'Absolutely! What would you like?'

Seb lunged for the menu. 'This may take a while.'

'Shall we get the Japanese sharing plate?' Hannah said to Maria. She liked the look of the rice, eggs, salmon and avocado.

'It looks kinda expensive . . .' Maria whispered back from across the table.

She waved her hand. 'It's cool, don't worry. My dad's work is paying for it. This week is technically a business trip.'

'*Thank you,*' Maria mouthed.

'Mmm.' Seb set the menu down. 'I want to try some Japanese food too.'

The waitress smiled. 'Have you ever tried sushi? That is the most famous Japanese food.' Seb shook his head and she pretended to whisper, 'The chef doesn't usually make it for breakfast, but I can ask him very nicely . . .'

Hannah grinned. 'Go on, you have to try it now!'

'Yeah!' said Maria. 'I tried vegetable sushi once and it was so tiny and cool.'

'All right, then.' Seb slotted his menu back in its holder. 'Looks like I have no choice!'

The waitress soon returned to the table with cutlery.

'Ah, jeez,' said Maria, staring at the two long metal sticks she'd been presented with.

'Chopsticks!' Hannah chuckled. 'I've never eaten breakfast with them before!'

'They're kinda my arch nemesis,' said Maria, grabbing one end of them. She moved the chopsticks up and down and grimaced. 'I suppose I've gotta learn how to use them one day.' Her hand slipped and a stick crashed on to her plate. 'Damn it!'

CHAPTER 4
SARDINE TIN

Soon, Hannah, Seb and Maria were tucking into their breakfast, Maria still battling with her chopsticks. The cafe was noisy with tourists and sports fans, so Hannah had to lean across the table to tell the others her idea.

'We need to find out where athletes go straight after their medal ceremony. It's the first place to look for clues.'

'Why don't we just go to the stadium and see?' Seb suggested, in between mouthfuls of sushi.

Hannah looked confused. 'How?'

'I can think of two possible ways.' He set down his chopsticks. 'One, we ask the volunteers and security guards working inside the stadium. Two, we—'

'Try to get access to the athletes' area ourselves,' Hannah interrupted. 'See if there are any doors that a thief could sneak in or out of.'

Seb nodded. 'Exactly.'

Hannah turned to Maria. 'You have that special pass, don't you?'

Maria reached for her belt bag. 'I've got four all-access passes for me and my family.' They get us into Block A in every venue – that's the VIP block. She showed them two passes. 'I have one spare as my dad had a migraine this morning, so he didn't go with Mom and Isabella to the Sportpark.'

'That's a shame,' said Hannah. 'Although it works for us . . . I already have a ticket for today, but do you, Seb?'

He shook his head, his cheeks bulging with food. Covering his mouth, he explained, 'But my dad was meant to be showing me round the media centre.' He scratched his head. 'I'll need to get out of that somehow.'

Maria slipped the passes back into her bag. 'Well, if you do, you can have my spare pass.' She nudged Seb with her elbow. 'You'll just have to pretend to be my brother.'

'Not a problem,' Seb boasted, stroking an imaginary beard. 'I'm a master of impressions.'

'Yeah? Prove it!' said Maria, folding her arms.

'Okay, then.' Seb hopped down from his chair and found himself some space between the tables. 'Guess who this is . . .'

He started by pretending to comb a moustache, before miming sitting a hat on his head. Hannah smiled as he turned out his feet and bent his knees. She watched Seb walk around in a little circle, twiddling an imaginary cane.

'I've got it!' She laughed.

Maria leaned across the table and confessed, 'I'm glad you do, because I have no idea!'

Seb jumped back into his seat. 'So . . . who was it?'

'Charlie Chaplin!' answered Hannah, then quickly panicked. 'It was, wasn't it?'

'Of course it was!'

Maria looked around. 'Charlie who?'

'Charlie Chaplin,' Seb explained. 'He was an actor in the nineteen twenties.'

'All the way up to the fifties!' added Hannah.

'How do *you* know so much about this Chaplin guy?' Maria asked her.

Hannah pointed to her outfit. 'My favourite era is the thirties! I love retro movies and clothes.'

Seb's eyes lit up. 'That's epic!'

Hannah felt a hand on her back and heard the sound of her dad's voice.

'She's not going on about vintage clothes, is she?'

'Dad!' Hannah shook her head at him.

Behind them, a flock of tourists gathered by the window for a group photo.

'Have you been enjoying the view?' Hannah's dad asked.

'Absolutely!' she replied, even though they'd barely looked outside, too focused on Jesse's medal. 'But I would like to see some more . . .'

Hannah's dad ushered everyone out of their seats. 'Well, if you come over to the other side, you'll have an amazing view of Mount Fuji.'

The four of them hurried over to the window and stared out into the distance. The sky was so clear that Hannah could see the top of the famous mountain.

'Wow!' Seb exclaimed. 'It's epic – and a lot bigger than I thought it'd be!'

Maria gawped. 'Imagine how long it would take to get to the top . . .'

Hannah opened up her satchel. 'I need to take a photo of this!'

'I'll take it for you, so you can all be in it,' said her dad. Hannah nodded and passed him her camera. 'Everybody, smile!'

Maria was the last to move into shot. She mumbled

to Seb out of the corner of her mouth, 'My mom makes us pose for so many photos.'

'So you must be a natural?' Seb replied.

'Not really...'

'Right,' said Hannah, stepping back from the window. She made a rectangle with her fingers and held it up to her eyes. 'Let's see... Right a bit, Seb...' She looked through her pretend lens. 'Maria, just one step to your left...' Maria shuffled along and Hannah gave her a thumbs up. 'Perfect!' She took her place in the middle of the photo and knelt down so the mountain was visible in the background.

Her dad laughed. 'Happy with the set-up, dear?' Hannah nodded. 'Okay, then. Say cheese!'

Seb grinned. 'Cheeeeese!'

As soon as the shutter had clicked, Hannah jumped up to take a look at the picture. 'Mmm...' She hesitated. 'Can we try one more, please?' Walking back to the window, she calculated, 'I'll stand next to Maria so we can see all of Mount Fuji...'

Her dad angled the camera again and pressed the button. 'This one's a winner!'

Click.

Hannah ran to assess the second photo. 'Mmm...'

Both Seb and Maria wandered over to take a look.

'That's a great shot!' said Maria. 'I'd frame that and hang it in my room.'

'What's wrong?' Seb asked Hannah.

'Does it look too staged? Maybe I should be on the other side...' She took another glance at the mountain. 'Maybe the camera angle is too high...'

Maria shook her head. 'It's perfect! And do you know why?' Hannah shook her head. 'Because you can see how happy we are! My mum always says that a photo is a way of capturing a moment, and this photo does that perfectly.'

Hannah's dad smiled. 'Those are very wise words, Maria.'

'I'll tell her that!'

Hannah took the camera back with a smile. 'I guess it doesn't have to be perfect.'

'You and perfect!' Her dad chuckled to himself. He took a look at his watch. 'Oh goodness! It's almost half nine! We need to get going if we want to make the shot-put heats.'

'But what about Seb and Maria?' She winked to the others. 'Can they come with us? Maria has a spare pass Seb can use.'

Her dad hesitated. 'Well, we'll have to check with your parents.'

Seb nodded and took his phone from his shirt pocket. 'I'll ring my dad!'

'My mom is probably waiting for me at the bottom of the tower, so we could go and ask her?' Maria said. 'I was meant to meet her five minutes ago . . .'

'We'd better hurry, then,' said Hannah's dad. He led the girls over to the lift and Seb trailed after them while he spoke to his dad.

'Okay, thanks, Dad! I'll see you later . . . Bye!' He hung up.

'What did he say?' asked Hannah.

The lift doors opened before Seb could answer, and everyone piled inside. Hannah pressed the button for level five and pointed to a little screen. 'I love how it tells you what floor you're on. It changes so fast!'

The doors closed and the lift began to move down, quickly.

'It's like being on a roller coaster!' said Maria.

Seb gave a nervous laugh. 'Yeah, a one-way roller coaster in a sardine tin.'

Hannah noticed him fiddling with the buttons on his shirt. 'You okay?'

He shrugged. 'I don't mind adrenaline kicks, but maybe falling three hundred and forty metres in a box with no windows is my limit.'

'You could pretend this is a stunt for the new James Bond movie?'

'Yeah!' said Maria. 'At least you're not standing *on top* of the elevator as the villain cuts through the wires.'

Seb's eyes almost burst from his head.

'Too much?' Hannah asked.

He nodded.

'Hang in there, buddy,' Hannah's dad said. 'There isn't long left.'

Hannah changed the subject to distract him. 'So what did your dad say?'

'He said I can spend the day with you.'

'Great!'

'As long as I'm done by three o'clock. My dad needs to be back at the hotel for a team briefing at four.'

'No problem,' said Hannah's dad. 'We can get you back by then.'

'Really? My dad said he can pick me up after work.'

'It's no problem, and we'll take Maria back too – as long as her parents say yes!'

'Thanks, Mr Walker!' she replied.

'Ow!' cried Seb. 'I just felt my ears pop!'

Hannah checked the screen. 'Only fifty floors left!'

'Forty-nine, forty-eight, forty-seven, forty-six...' Maria counted.

Eventually, the lift came to a stop and an automated voice announced, '*Level five. Doors opening.*'

Maria gave Seb a pat on the back. 'You can relax now.'

They all stepped out of the lift and into the fresh air. Hannah squinted in the sunlight. 'That's bright!'

Her dad breathed in deeply and grinned. 'That's because the sun is shining!' He slid on his sunglasses. 'Isn't it lovely and warm?'

Hannah rolled her eyes. Her dad was always stating the obvious!

Being back on the ground was weird, remembering

how small it had all looked from Floor 340. The white apartment buildings were towering over her. The zebra crossings on the road seemed to stretch on for ever.

Maria was waving to her mum, who was standing at a nearby bus stop. She ran over and gave Maria a hug.

'Did you have fun?' she asked her.

'Loads!' She paused. 'Mom, I have something to ask . . .'

As Maria asked her mum if she could spend the day with her friends, Seb wandered over to Hannah.

'What shall we call our investigation?'

Before Hannah could make a suggestion, Maria came running over. 'She said yes!'

'Great!' Hannah said. 'Any ideas for what we should call the case?'

'Ooh, yay!' said Maria. 'We're gonna give it a name.'

'How about "The Gold Medal Mystery"?' said Hannah.

Maria chuckled. 'It sounds like a book.'

'Or an epic film,' said Seb. He raised his hand. 'I vote *The Gold Medal Mystery*.'

He turned to Maria, who was nodding. 'If they turn it into a movie once we're heroes, they'll already have a name for it.'

'Seb, you could play yourself!' Hannah joked.

'That'd be epic! And Maria could do the Portuguese translation.'

Maria shook her head. 'Oh no. I can't listen to the sound of my own voice.'

Behind them, Hannah's dad said goodbye to Carmella. 'We'll drop Maria back this afternoon.'

'Thanks, Michael,' she said to Hannah's dad, and waved to Maria. 'Have a good time!'

Hannah's dad held out his hand for an oncoming bus that displayed SPORTPARK on the front. As it pulled into the stop, her dad reminded the three of them, 'I've got your parents' phone numbers if they want to contact me.' The doors opened and he ushered them on board. 'And make sure to let me know if you need anything. Food, drink, whatever you need.'

They thanked him and the four of them hopped on to the bus.

'Cool kids at the back!' Seb ran to the back and claimed the middle seat.

Maria and Hannah chased after him.

'Let's go and find this medal!' whispered Hannah as the bus pulled off.

CHAPTER 5
SMOOTHIE SURPRISE

When the bus pulled up beside the path to the stadium, a huge crowd of people were gathered, carrying flags and banners, and singing a series of chants. Maria leaped off the bus. 'Look at all those signs!' she gasped.

Seb squinted. 'Who do you think they're here to see?'

'No idea. It's kinda weird cos the athletes' entrance is on the other side of the stadium.'

They made their way down the path and Hannah began to make out parts of the chant.

'. . . OF SPORT . . . CROWN . . . FOUND . . .'

As they approached, she saw most of the flags were American ones, just like the one that Maria had given to Jesse. She concentrated to hear more of the chant.

'THE . . . OF SPORT . . . HIS CROWN! THE . . . THIEF MUST BE FOUND!'

47

'They're protesting about the thief!' Hannah exclaimed.

Seb grabbed her arm. 'Do you think other people are trying to find the medal too?'

'I just want Jesse to have his medal back,' Maria said. 'So maybe it's a good thing if loads of people are looking for it, not just us?'

'Careful!' Hannah spun round to check if her dad had heard Maria, but he was too busy looking at the queue for the ticket desk. 'You got away with that!' She winked, then lowered her voice. 'And it's our mystery,' she whispered. 'We have to find the thief first!'

Hannah's dad steered them round the protesters. 'This way,' he said. 'Let's not get in their path.'

As the others walked on, Hannah stopped next to a girl holding a sign on a stick. She was being interviewed by an American reporter. *That'll encourage even more people to start looking*, she thought. It was great for Jesse, but it gave her, Maria and Seb plenty of rivals for that reward.

She caught up with everyone at the ticket desk. She opened up her satchel and handed her ticket to a smiley volunteer in a bright blue uniform.

'Enjoy!' He stamped it and returned it to Hannah. The man then turned to Maria and Seb, with their all-access passes. 'Hmm . . .' He frowned.

Hannah's heart sank. Was he going to question Seb's pass? After all, it had Maria's surname on it, not his.

But his frown turned to a grin. 'I'm so jealous! I want one of these!'

Hannah saw Seb sigh with relief and begin to laugh.

'If you want it, you'll have to pretend to be her brother!' Seb pointed to Maria.

'You are very lucky!'

'I have a very talented sister!' he replied, 'She's a long jumper and won these! But don't you get to see the events too?'

The volunteer waved his hand. 'Sometimes. If the qualifiers are still happening after I finish work.'

'Oh, that's not fair.'

'It's okay! I just like being a part of the Games!'

Hannah had never seen anyone so happy to be working. 'You must really love your job!'

'The chance to do this is once in a lifetime!' He beamed.

Of course, Hannah thought. Having the Games in their home city was a really special thing for the Tokyo people.

'I hope you have an amazing Games!' she said.

'You too! It was nice to meet you all.'

The four of them waved goodbye and began to move on towards security, but the volunteer suddenly rushed after them.

'Wait!' he cried, reaching into his pocket. 'Erm . . . I want you to have these.' He presented Hannah, Seb and Maria with three little objects from the palm of his hand. 'Because you are so kind.'

'Cool – pin badges!' squealed Hannah, taking one. 'Thank you so much!'

He nodded. 'Yes, official Tokyo pin badges!'

The others took their gifts and smiled.

'Thanks a lot!' said Maria, attaching the pin to her pass.

'You're welcome!' The volunteer waved goodbye. 'I have to work now. See you another time!'

'My training partner told me that each country has their own team badge,' Maria said as they approached security. 'People collect them and swap them, which is kinda awesome.'

Hannah stashed her badge in her satchel. 'The athletes must get loads of cool stuff!'

'Apparently, four years ago, one of the American swimmers got a pin badge from the refugee team!'

Hannah stopped behind the queue for security checks. 'That's amazing!'

Up ahead, a security guard shouted, 'Bags and coats on the conveyor belt, please!'

The stadium security check reminded Hannah of the scanners at the airport. Only smaller and in a little hut outside the stadium. She placed her satchel in a tray. Maria and Seb did the same with their belongings and walked through the scanners. On the other side, they picked up their bags and continued inside through the main doors. Hannah could suddenly feel her heart pounding. They weren't just here to watch sports today. They were here to find a thief.

But as she looked around, her initial fears were coming true. The stadium was like a maze. Encircling every level was a corridor of food and drink stands, with sets of stairs on opposite sides. There were gift shops and toilets, and she knew the stadium had three levels!

'Where do we even start?' she muttered.

'This way, everyone!' said her dad, pointing to the stairs. 'We don't have much time before the final begins.'

Hannah looked at Seb and Maria. They needed an excuse to start investigating – and fast.

'Can we go to the gift shop first?' She pointed at the one she could see nearby. 'I didn't have time yesterday.'

Her dad checked his watch. 'Now?'

Hannah nodded. 'Don't worry, you don't have to come!' She knew her dad wouldn't want to miss a minute of the shot put. 'We'll come and find you afterwards.'

He shook his head, bemused. 'Okay, then. Your seat number is on your ticket, so you'll be able to find me from that – it's right next to mine, in Block H.'

The three of them smiled.

'Thanks, Dad!' said Hannah, and they hurried towards the shop.

As soon as they were inside the busy shop, Seb rushed off towards the official Tokyo Games merchandise.

'Didn't Seb realize you just used the shop as an excuse to get away?' Maria said, pushing up her glasses. 'Should we go after him?'

Hannah rolled her eyes. 'I don't see him coming back any time soon otherwise.'

They joined Seb by the baskets full of mini Games mascots. The plush toys ranged from 'Mini Yui' to 'Lifesize Yui', which was almost the same size as Hannah.

Maria crept up behind him and tutted over his shoulder. 'You're not going to find the medal in there . . .'

'Woah!' Seb cried, startled, tripping into a heap of mini Yuis.

As Maria helped him back up, Hannah spotted a

rotating stand full of leaflets.

Behind her, she heard Seb dust himself down and ask, 'So where do we start?'

Hannah pulled a map from the stand. 'This should give us an idea.' She unfolded it over her leg. 'The font's a little small . . .' She passed it to Maria and Seb, who held it out between them.

Maria scanned the tiny symbols. 'What exactly are we looking for?'

'Anywhere Jesse may have been yesterday,' Hannah said. 'Changing rooms, prep rooms . . .' She gestured to Seb. 'Media rooms? You know something about those, right?'

Seb shook his head. 'I've only ever been to a media centre. I've never actually been into the stadium press rooms.'

Maria took another look at the map and sighed. 'I can only see places for spectators.'

'Ugh!' Hannah rubbed her face with her hand. 'Never mind. The map was a stupid idea anyway!' She refolded the map and returned it to the stand.

'Your idea wasn't stupid,' Seb reassured Hannah. 'We just need another way to find out where Jesse was yesterday.'

People were crowding into the shop now, and a lady squashed Maria into a shelf of action figures as she tried to pass. She shook her head. 'Can we go somewhere quieter? Your dad will have gone by now.'

They left the shop and took a seat by one of the concourse food stalls. Hannah opened up her satchel for a drink, panting. 'Wow, I'm thirsty! It's so hot here.'

'Oh shoot!' said Maria. 'I left my water bottle in the hotel.'

'No worries!' Seb said. 'I'll get you a drink with the pass.'

'Huh?' Maria said, looking confused.

Seb showed her the bottom of his pass. 'You know this gets us free smoothies?'

'How do you know that?'

He grinned. 'The small print on the back!'

Maria flipped her pass over. 'Ah! I can't believe I missed that.'

Seb walked over to the menu on the wall. 'Berry, tropical, or smoothie surprise?'

'Berry, please!'

'Seb, wait!' Hannah said as an idea popped into her head. She hurried over to the counter. 'Ask the volunteer about what's downstairs!'

'Good idea!' He nodded towards the menu. 'Do you want anything?'

'Berry too, please.'

She sat back down next to Maria and started to listen in to the conversation between Seb and the volunteer when the man at the stand fired up the blender and his voice went muffled.

Hannah turned to Maria and laughed. 'I guess we won't be eavesdropping, then. I can't hear a thing!'

After about thirty seconds, the volunteer switched the blender off and handed Seb the smoothies.

'Thank you,' Seb said before returning to his seat.

Maria looked at him with wide eyes. 'So?' she asked.

Seb slid the cup along the table. 'He said he doesn't know and that I'd get into a lot of trouble if I tried to go down there.'

Hannah rested her head on her hand. 'Okay, well is there anyone else we can ask?'

The friends stared out to the concourse and watched a group of excited girls in blue-and-white kimonos run into the gift shop.

'Hey!' said Seb. 'I recognize those outfits.'

'They're flower girls in the medal ceremonies,' said Maria.

'What are they doing up here?' Hannah wondered.

'Probably visiting the shop before the five thousand metres finishes and even more people crowd inside,' said Maria.

'Do you remember the schedule by heart?' Hannah asked.

'Yeah, I guess I kinda do.'

'All right, then,' said Seb, 'when is the women's steeplechase?'

Maria counted out the days on her hand. 'The heats are tomorrow, but the final is in four days.'

'Is there an American in it?' Seb asked.

'A few . . .' She shook her head. 'But the main medal contenders are from Uganda.'

Seb nodded approvingly. 'Wow, you're like a walking encyclopaedia!'

While the others were chatting, Hannah had a brainwave. Maybe these flower girls were also at Jesse's medal ceremony! And they'd know where the athletes went afterwards at least.

She explained her plan to try to speak to them.

'Ooh, quick thinking!' Seb said, throwing his backpack on and making his way to the gift-shop door.

Maria followed behind him. 'Let's hope it works . . .'

Hannah shook her head. 'It needs to, after my other ideas!'

They stopped outside and peered through the window.

'There they are!' whispered Maria, pointing to the group of girls.

They watched as their targets flicked through official Games comic books.

'Let's go,' said Seb, walking inside and over to the comic section. He picked up a book written entirely in Japanese, then waved at the girls. 'Hello!'

'Hello!' the girls replied, smiling.

'Do you know about the medal prep room?'

The girls looked at him blankly.

'Did you see Jesse yesterday?'

They turned to each other and began speaking in Japanese.

Hannah got out her phone and brought up the translation app. She quickly typed, *Were you at Jesse's medal ceremony yesterday?*

She showed the girl in front of her the Japanese translation and smiled.

The group took one look at the app and shrugged.

Maybe it's too complicated, Hannah thought. 'Hold on a second . . .' She typed out a new, simpler question.

Did you see Jesse yesterday?

She looked up and held out her phone, but the girls had already scattered themselves around the shop. This wasn't going to work, she realized.

'Stupid app!' Hannah huffed, stuffing her phone back into her pocket.

Seb turned away from the shelf where he'd returned the comic. 'So, uh . . . what now?'

CHAPTER 6
MEXICAN WAVE

'Maybe we should head upstairs to your dad and watch the shot put?' Seb suggested.

'But we've only just started!' Maria complained.

Hannah couldn't face the thought of failure either. The shop was emptying now, so she wandered over to a Tokyo Games patio set in the corner.

'I've never given up on anything before and I don't want to start now.'

She pulled up a garden chair, and Maria and Seb followed.

'But we do need to go into the arena,' she said, lowering her satchel from her shoulder.

'Ah, really?' Maria stared down at her feet. 'I don't want to let Jesse down.'

Hannah placed her notebook on the table, opened it

to a new page and drafted a new heading. 'We're not going to let him down.'

'How can we help Jesse if we're sitting in the stands?'

'Because –' Hannah put her pen down – 'we're not actually going to watch the shot put.'

Seb frowned. 'Not even a little bit?'

She shook her head. 'Sorry, but not until we've found the medal.'

'So we're not stopping the search?' Maria grinned.

'No – we're going into the arena to get as close to the track as we can.'

Seb read the new heading in her notebook. '*Track Investigation?*'

'Yes. We'll be able to see from there how the athletes get to the underground level. There must be a door that they go through.' Hannah turned to Maria. 'Can your passes get us some seats at the front?'

She nodded. 'Only in Block A, where we sat yesterday. It's on the other side of the stadium.'

Hannah shoved her notebook back into her bag and stood up. 'Cool! Then let's go!'

'But your tickets are for Block H!' Maria reminded Hannah.

'I'll figure something out.'

As they left the shop Seb gasped, 'No way!'

Hannah spun round. 'What?'

'The karaoke machine is ninety-six thousand yen!'

Maria grabbed his hand and hurried him along. 'We can buy it when we find the medal!'

The three of them raced along the concourse, weaving in and out of spectators, Maria leading the way. Hannah was impressed. Maria was unbelievably quick when she ran at full speed. If it hadn't been for the crowds of people, she would have left them for dust! Before she knew it, Hannah was staring at the arched entrance to Block A.

'Right,' Hannah said, dragging the other two to one side. 'I have an idea to get us all in.' She turned to Seb. 'Seb, can you give me your pass for a moment, please?'

He handed it over and she smiled.

The others watched as Hannah unclipped the pass from its official Tokyo lanyard and handed it back. Balancing the lanyard on her knee, Hannah clipped the ends together and hung it around her neck. 'If I tuck the clipped ends inside my jacket, it looks like I'm wearing a normal pass.'

She knelt down and pulled the laces from her shoes. 'Do your shirt up,' she instructed Seb, as she passed the ribbons to Maria. 'Could you tie these in a loop to hang round his neck?'

'Ooh, I see what you're doing!' said Maria.

Once she'd finished tying, Maria handed Hannah the makeshift lanyard, and she attached it to Seb's pass and hung it around his neck.

'Now, tuck this under your shirt,' she ordered.

Seb gave a nod of approval as he did so. 'Epic job!' The shirt was just short enough for the pass to be peeking out at the bottom.

Hannah brushed her trousers, feeling pretty pleased with herself.

'Nice! Now it looks like we're both wearing passes.' She stole a glance at the two volunteers under the archway checking people's tickets. 'Right . . .' She took a deep breath. 'Let's go.'

'We've got this,' said Seb. Hannah relaxed into a smile, and he gave her a nudge. 'After all, we're the dream team.'

The three of them headed over to the entrance. As they approached, one of the female volunteers held out a hand.

'Tickets, please.'

'We have these actually,' Seb replied, flashing his pass.

The volunteer's eyes widened. 'Ooh! Lucky you!' She and her colleague both stepped aside and let them into the stand.

Hannah grinned. 'Thank you!'

They descended the stairs and Seb tapped Hannah on the shoulder. 'See, nothing to worry about.'

Hannah gasped and dived behind a row of seats.

'What is it?' asked Maria, looking around.

Hannah gestured them closer. 'I can see my dad!' She pointed to the level above them, where her dad was sitting in the front row.

Maria and Seb ducked down too.

'What's the problem?' asked Seb, peering over Maria's shoulder.

'If my dad sees us, he'll want to know why we're down here.'

'We can come up with an excuse.'

'He'd still be suspicious,' she shouted over the crowd. 'And if he works out we're trying to find the medal, there's no way he'll let us snoop around.'

Maria pulled a face. 'Yeah, that is a problem.'

Seb crept along the row and grabbed a Japanese flag that had been abandoned across the seats. 'We can hide under this.'

Sandwiching Maria in the middle, Hannah took one end of the flag.

'It's a little small,' she said, shuffling closer.

'You'll have to squeeze, then!' Seb teased.

She began to sidestep along the row. 'I think I can make this work...'

Maria and Seb followed until they were all stood together on the stairs.

'One of us needs to stay a step behind,' Hannah said. 'It's too narrow for us all to go down together.'

Maria nodded. 'I can do tha—'

Before she could finish, Hannah was already two steps down. She hurried to catch up, but was soon on the same step as Seb. 'Quick!' Maria urged him, as Hannah panicked.

'Seb, get down here!'

Seb rushed to join Hannah, but as he did so, she saw the flag began to slip from Maria's back.

'Wait! Seb, slow down!' Hannah shouted. 'Maria is about to be exposed!' They came to a halt and the trio found themselves bunched together on the same step.

Maria chuckled to herself. 'Well, that could have gone better . . .'

Hannah caught sight of Seb talking to a boy at the end of the row.

'Psst . . . Hey . . .' The boy looked up at Seb hunched under the flag. 'Do you reckon you can start a Mexican wave?'

The boy rolled his eyes. 'Easy! Watch this . . .'

It looked like Seb had picked the right person for the job. While the boy got the attention of the people around him, Seb told the others, 'When I say "go", we need to drop the flag, run down the steps and take a seat in the front row.'

Maria looked around. 'Wait, what?'

The boy yelled, 'Now!' to the people in the stands, who all got to their feet and lifted their arms into the air.

'Go!' yelled Seb.

He, Hannah and Maria dashed to a cluster of empty front-row seats.

As they sat down, they watched the wave ripple around the entire stadium. As it reached the halfway point, even fans in the upper levels joined in!

'I have to say, that was an amazing distraction!' said Hannah.

Maria sat open-mouthed. 'How did you . . . get all those people . . .' She gave a nod of approval. 'Well done, Sebastian.'

They had another stroke of luck when the women's shot-put qualifiers began to heat up at the far end of the stadium. All eyes were on Oksana Mereshko as she prepared for the second throw of the morning. Hannah looked up at the scoreboard and saw that her first attempt was two centimetres off the world record. Her own world record. Mereshko waved to the crowd from the circle and everyone began to clap their hands. The clap made its way round the stadium and Seb was the first to join in.

'Come on!' he said. 'We can watch this throw and then carry on with our investigation.'

The clapping got faster and Maria joined in. 'Only because she might break the world record.'

Hannah sat thinking about how to get on to the track. They could try to sneak over the barrier, but with at least two volunteers in every stand and what seemed like all the world's cameras, they were bound to be caught.

'Hey, Hannah!'

She turned to Seb.

'Why aren't you joining in?'

'Because I'm trying to think!'

'Enjoy the shot put!' He laughed. 'Then we'll figure it out together!'

Hannah reluctantly tapped her leg in time with the beat. Mereshko raised a hand into the air and the clapping grew even faster. Hannah kept stamping her foot in time to the claps and watched Mereshko nestle the shot into her neck. The noise of the crowd rolled around the stadium like thunder. With two steps to the right, the Ukrainian launched the shot into the air. It soared over the ten-metre mark, then the fifteen-metre.

As the shot neared the twenty-metre line, Maria leaned over the barrier. 'Jeez, it's good!'

It hit the ground just past the line and Mereshko let out a cheer. She knew it was good. Just how good was it?

The officials ran over with their measuring equipment.

Hannah asked Maria, 'What's the record?'

'It's 22.63 metres.'

Hannah looked at the shot. It was over twenty metres. She stared up at the scoreboard and waited for the result to come in: 22.64 metres!

Mereshko had done it!

The whole stadium got to their feet and applauded

Oksana Mereshko as she ran over to her coach and wrapped her arms around her.

Seb gave Hannah a nudge. 'See! It was worth watching.'

'I guess you're right . . .' she confessed over the cheers. As they sat back down she spotted a volunteer standing by the gate to the photography pen. 'Hey, I have an idea.'

Maria leaned forward. 'Yeah?'

'Should we ask that man if we can get on the track? You know, to hand Mereshko a flag or something?'

Maria gestured to the first heat of the five-thousand-metre race. 'We won't get far with that going on.'

'We don't need to actually go on the track. We can go around it and find a way to the athletes' section.'

'You really think they'll let us all the way round?'

Hannah studied the route around the stadium. There weren't just guards down there, but also so many photographers, in place for the different events. 'Wait! They'll have photos of everything!'

'What?' said Seb.

'Yesterday, the photographers wouldn't have taken their eyes off Jesse. They'll know which door he entered the stadium through and which one he used to leave!'

'And,' Seb added, 'they'll be able to tell us where the medal prep room is!'

'Exactly!' said Hannah. 'At last we'll know.'

Maria nodded. 'Photographers do get everywhere.'

Hannah picked up her satchel and got to her feet. 'Come on, let's go and ask.'

The three of them shuffled along the front row until they reached the tall, rather burly volunteer.

Hannah did her best to get his attention. She climbed up on to the railing, so that they were the same height. 'Uh, excuse me . . .' she said.

'Get down from there, miss,' the volunteer growled.

She clambered down and he was towering over her once more. 'Oh, sorry. I don't suppose we could speak to some of the photographers could we? I'm an amateur photographer and I want to get some tips!' she lied.

The man scowled without looking at her and shook his head. 'Just return to your seat.'

'We have these passes!' She lifted hers up.

He examined the pass. 'Oh, I see! Aspiring athlete!'

'So can we get past?'

He let out an ugly laugh. 'Come back to me when you have proper athlete accreditation, my dear.'

Over her shoulder Hannah heard Maria hiss, 'Oh, I will . . .'

CHAPTER 7
MUSHINKEI

Hannah walked away from the volunteer, shaking her head. 'Let's just go.'

Maria pointed to the ring of volunteers encircling the track. 'There are people in blue everywhere. Perhaps we just picked the wrong one.'

'I suppose we could ask that one in Block D.' Hannah gestured to a girl using a giant beach ball to play catch with the crowd, who looked far more approachable. 'She's far away enough to not be seen by my dad.'

'She's perfect,' Maria whispered.

Seb disappeared down the row to plan their escape route. Hannah watched as Seb chatted to the same boy from earlier, motioning with his hands. Within seconds a Mexican wave was on its way round the stadium. While Hannah's dad was distracted, the three friends bolted up the stairs.

'Follow me!' Hannah led the others back out to the concourse.

Behind her, she could hear Seb chanting, 'Left, right, left, right . . .'

She spun round and came to a stop.

'Left, ri— Ow!' Seb marched straight into the back of Maria. 'Why did we stop?'

'Why are you marching?' Hannah asked.

'Because you are leading us into our mission.'

'I'm not the leader!'

Secretly, Hannah quite liked being group leader. But she didn't want her new friends to think that she was bossy.

Seb made his way over to the drinks stand. 'You're good at it!' he said. 'I bet you've got loads to put in your notebook!'

They each took a seat. Hannah pulled out her notebook, even though she didn't really want to prove Seb right.

'So what are you writing down?' asked Maria.

'Did that guard seem suspicious to you?' Hannah said, turning to her *Track Investigation* page.

'If *suspicious* is another word for *rude*.'

71

Seb nodded. 'He was more serious than everyone else...
All the volunteers here seem so nice. Like the guy who gave
us the pins, and the girl playing ball with the crowd.'

Hannah jotted down what had happened. 'What if
the mean guard was hired after Jesse's medal was stolen?'

'There's nothing stopping them bringing in nice
people,' Maria grumbled.

Hannah noted it down. 'Maybe they're trying to scare
people out of stealing anything else?'

'Or scare people from trying to win the reward money...'
They both turned to Seb. He raised his hands in defence.
'I don't know! It was just a suggestion.'

Hannah wrote it down anyway. 'We need to keep our
options open!'

Seb laughed. 'Your options are so open, you'll need a
new notebook soon!'

She snapped the book shut and slotted it back in her
satchel. 'I'm making sure we don't miss anything!' She
took a drink from her bottle. 'Now, let's find someone
more useful.'

They set off down the concourse in the direction of
Block D. As they arrived at the entrance, Maria stopped.

'Shoot, my passes only get us into Block A!'

Seb kept walking. 'Follow me.'

Hannah and Maria followed him inside the stand.

'Tickets, please!' a volunteer said, smiling.

Seb returned the smile. 'We have these special passes, you see. But Block A is all full up.'

The volunteer took a look over at the packed stand and put her finger to her lips. 'Shh, don't tell anybody, but you can come in here.'

'Thank you! We really are grateful. We've been desperate to see Oksana Mereshko all week!'

She gave him a pat on the back as he, Maria and Hannah hurried through the entrance.

'Nice one!' Maria whispered. She spotted the chatty volunteer. 'There she is!'

'After sweet-talking us in here, I think Seb should handle this one,' said Hannah.

'Agreed!' Maria said.

Seb wandered down the steps and over to the front row of seats. At least he didn't have to hide under a flag this time, Hannah thought as she watched him reach a lady on the end of the row and gift her a gigantic smile.

'Hi there . . .' The posh British accent he was putting on was one that Hannah had only heard her mum's diplomat friends use. 'I'm terribly sorry, but would we be able to get past? I'm afraid our seats are a little further down.'

The lady and her family rushed to their feet and let them all through. 'Of course!' she replied. As they shuffled along, Hannah saw that the entire row had made space for them. She thanked everyone as she passed.

'It's so cool how you can just change characters like that!' she told Seb when they reached the other end.

He took a bow. 'Accents are my favourite thing to do.'

Joining them on the steps, Maria joked, 'Are you as good at languages? Preferably Japanese!'

'Um . . . well, I know German! As for my Japanese, it's a work in progress . . .'

'So, you know some?'

He shook his head. 'Do *hello* and *goodbye* count?'

'You said it was a work in progress!'

He shrugged. 'You have to start somewhere.'

'Quick!' Hannah spotted the volunteer climbing the stairs. 'She looks like she's about to leave!'

Seb ran after her. 'I'm on it!' He gave her a tap on the shoulder and greeted her with a smile. 'I was just looking for a volunteer. I don't suppose that you could help me, could you?' He was back to full 'diplomat mode'.

She looked at her watch. 'Sure! I have about ten minutes to spare.'

'Oh, thank you!' Seb led the volunteer back down to

Hannah and Maria. 'I'm Seb, by the way.'

'I'm Sakura. It means *cherry blossom* in English.' She reached the bottom of the stairs and smiled at Hannah and Maria. 'What do you need help with?'

'We were wondering whether we could speak to some of the trackside press.' Seb gestured to a lady by the start line barking orders at a film crew. 'My friend Hannah is a pupil of that lady down there.'

Sakura sniggered. 'That lady?'

The four of them watched the formidable young woman as she yelled at a nearby cameraman and sent a make-up artist off in tears.

'That's Machi Mari! The most famous film director in Japan.' Sakura shook her head. 'She doesn't give advice to anybody. She tutors you?!'

Hannah awkwardly played with the buckle on her bag.

'Okay, so maybe my friend isn't a pupil of Machi . . .' Seb admitted. 'But she is an aspiring director!'

'A really good one too!' Maria lied.

'She's seen every film there is! From Alfred Hitchcock to Steven Spielberg!' Seb added.

Sakura seemed unsure.

'Her favourite is Charlie Chaplin!' Maria added.

Sakura broke her frown. 'Well, that is very sweet, but I can't let you on the track.'

Seb pointed to a member of Machi's crew who was crouched behind a computer. 'Is he downloading all the camera footage?'

'I don't know,' said Sakura. 'How do you know so much about it?'

'My dad is a TV presenter.'

'Oh, that's nice!'

Hannah looked at all the different cameras pointing across the stadium.

They must see everything, thought Hannah. She suddenly had a brainwave. 'Do they film behind the scenes?'

'Probably,' said Sakura. 'They're filming a documentary about the Games.' She lowered her voice. 'Apparently, Machi is favourite to be the Emperor of Japan's next official documentary-maker!'

'Who else might get it?' Seb asked.

'Oh.' Sakura cast out her hand. 'All big directors want it!'

Hannah turned to the track. 'In that case, there must be loads of documentaries going on right now!'

'Well, a Japanese swimmer said on TV that it was like living under surveillance!'

Not a moment would have been missed, thought Hannah. Which helped them!

'I bet Machi got loads of footage of Jesse yesterday, then,' Seb said.

Sakura shook her head. 'She wasn't here yesterday.'

'What?' Maria gasped. 'She missed it?'

'She was filming something at the tennis, I think...'

Hannah continued to watch Machi Mari, who was now leaning over the shoulder of her cameraman. She beckoned to a teenage girl with a snap of her fingers. 'Who's that?' Hannah asked, as a tall red-headed girl scurried over carrying a fancy white case with a gold star.

'That'll be her latest assistant.'

'Latest?' Seb said.

Sakura nodded. 'Oh yes – it's almost a different one each day! We place bets on who will be next.'

Hannah frowned. 'That's harsh.'

The volunteer laughed. 'Machi's harsh. We call her 'Mushinkei Mari. Mushinkei means *callous*, or as you would say, *mean*.'

Seb laughed. 'So in English it would be Meanie Mari?'

'Exactly.'

Maria winced as the assistant desperately rummaged for something inside the case. 'This doesn't look good . . .'

Machi snatched the bag from the girl's grasp and stormed off the track. Even from the stands, the four of them could hear her disgusted shrieking.

Sakura shook her head. 'Oh, looks like another one has gone.'

'How do you know so much?' Hannah asked.

'I've been watching Machi for years as a volunteer. She was a runner at the London Games and a camera assistant in Rio.'

Hannah smiled. 'You volunteered in London?'

Sakura nodded.

'That's why your English is so good.'

'I lived there as a girl, so it should be!' Sakura looked up at the time on the big screen. 'Ah, I'm sorry! I need to go.'

'Already?' replied Hannah.

'I'm sorry. If I see you another time, I'll give you a mini tour of the stadium.'

'Even the athletes' parts?!' Hannah took her chance.

Sakura laughed. 'My pass can't even go down there!'

'But is there someone who can take us?'

Sakura shook her head. 'I wish I knew someone who could.'

She waved goodbye to the friends. 'I'll see you around, though!'

The three of them waved back as she left the stand.

'We need to get our hands on yesterday's footage,' said Hannah. 'The thief must be on it somewhere.'

'And how do we find that?' said Maria.

'We need to find a camera crew — but it sounds like Machi's will be tricky . . .'

'My dad's team might have footage!' said Seb.

'But he was here with you yesterday,' Hannah.

'Yeah, because another presenter was working then. They must film everything too.'

Hannah started moving up the stairs. 'Let's find a table and write everything down.' She spun round. 'Oh and, Seb?'

'Yeah?'

'Could you ask your dad for all their footage of Jesse?'

'I'll find a way . . .'

'You could say you want to know how athletes behave behind the scenes, in case you have to play one,' Maria called out behind him.

'That's a good idea. I'll text him now.'

'Let's find somewhere to sit,' Hannah said as they emerged on to the concourse.

Seb popped his head up from his phone. 'Are you hungry?'

'Yeah, I kinda am,' Maria admitted.

Hannah scanned the level and saw a bright green sushi bar up ahead. 'We could grab some, okay?'

'Sure!' said Seb.

'I guess I've gotta practise my chopstick skills sometimes!' Maria added.

As the three of them headed towards the sushi bar, Seb's phone pinged with messages.

'What's your dad saying?' Hannah asked.

'Well . . . he can get some footage.'

'That's a start!'

'Wait, though – he also said that live TV only has access to the track and the press room. It's the documentary- and film-makers that have behind-the-scenes footage.'

'Ugh!' Hannah rubbed her face. 'This is becoming impossible!' The three of them stopped at the sushi bar and she slung her satchel on to a stool. 'It's like the universe doesn't want us to find the medal!'

CHAPTER 8
IT'S ONLY PENCIL

The friends each took a stool at the sushi bar. Hannah rested her elbows on the placemat.

'This is epic!'

Hannah looked over to see Seb playing with a keypad on the table. 'What does it do?'

'The keypad is how you order!'

Seb began punching numbers into it.

Hannah looked down and studied the display in front of her. She had a list of dishes on one side and her own keypad on the other – all in front of a moving conveyor belt. She looked around at the other diners running their fingers along the menu. She did the same with hers and realized that each dish was allocated its own number.

'It's not working!' Seb growled.

Maria leaned over and examined the problem.

'Okay, it's asking you to put money in first or scan your card.' Seb reached down for his backpack, but Maria held out her hand. 'I can get it with my pass!'

'Oh yeah!'

He popped back up and Maria scanned her pass's barcode. She leaned across and swiped it over Hannah's display too.

'Food for us all!'

Hannah pulled her notebook from her satchel. 'I'm going to make some notes. Can you order for me? Anything pescetarian is good.'

'Well, you've come to the right place.' Seb chuckled.

Hannah bit her fingernails as she tried to remember everything about their morning. After several pages of notes about the photographers, the suspicious guard and missing Machi at the ceremony, she looked up.

'Cool, my notes are up to date.'

'Good!' said Seb. 'Now you can watch this.'

'Watch what?'

Seb pointed to the ceiling of the sushi bar. 'You see how it's divided into squares?'

Hannah looked up and nodded.

'Well, each square is a hatch that dispenses food from the ceiling.'

Hannah watched as the number four hatch opened up and lowered a plate on to the moving conveyor belt.

'No way! That's amazing!'

She watched the plate make its way round to its owner, who picked it up and set it on the table in front of him.

The three friends were totally transfixed by the contraption.

'Ooh.' Seb waved his hands. 'Let's play a game!'

Hannah chuckled. 'Go on, then.'

'Guess which one is going to open next.'

Maria rolled her eyes. 'That's just luck! There's no skill in that.'

'Ah, well.' He shrugged. 'I pick number seven!'

Hannah studied the conveyor belt for clues. There were lots of crab rolls circulating, so she checked its number on the menu. 'I'll guess number four.'

'Two!' chose Maria. 'It's my lucky number.'

They stared up at the ceiling and waited for the all-important answer. Despite only playing a game, Hannah held her breath, desperate to be right.

There was a small whirring sound up above and Seb performed a mini drum roll. 'The moment of truth . . .'

A hatch on the left began to move and Hannah's eyes darted across.

'Yes!' She let her breath out. 'Number four!'

Maria turned to her and gawped. 'Was that a guess? Or did you actually know?'

Hannah pointed to the conveyor belt. 'I picked the most popular dish. Better odds!'

Seb slapped his head. 'Ah no! I ordered it!'

The girls collapsed into giggles as he picked up the plate. He stretched over and passed it to Hannah. 'I got it for you. Our order must be coming through now!'

She took the crab rolls and smiled. 'Ah, you were thwarted by your own selflessness. Thank you.'

'You're welcome.'

Between them, Maria kept an eye out for more orders. 'Another one!'

Seb lunged for the plates as they passed. He quickly handed them to Maria, who sorted them between the friends.

After the flurry of food, Maria surveyed the collection. 'Hmm, I think that's everything.'

Hannah looked at what appeared to be about ten little plates scattered in front of her. She rolled her eyes. 'Seb, I thought we were having a quick snack!'

'Pfft, I can eat fast!'

Maria set a bottle of hand gel on to the table and joked, 'Fast or not, we're going to need this.'

She offered the sanitizer to Seb, who took hold of the bottle and shook it upside down ... but the entire cap flew off. Hannah's book was hit with a smattering of hand gel.

'No!' She jumped up and tried to save the smudging ink.

Seb came running over with a stack of napkins. 'I'm so sorry!'

She tore the ruined page from her book and sighed. 'It's okay – I'll redo it.'

'I'll do it. I made the mess.'

Hannah took out her pen. 'Nah, it's fine.'

Seb tidied up the last traces of hand gel and joked, 'Look on the bright side! Everything's now very clean.'

Hannah grimaced. 'That's true!'

The others tucked into their sushi as Hannah finished copying out the soggy page. It wasn't a bad thing that she'd had to go over the clues twice, she told herself.

'So why wasn't Machi at the track yesterday?' Maria said.

'Apparently she was filming the tennis,' Hannah answered.

'But why would she miss Haru's final? He's the most famous athlete on the Japanese team!'

Hannah ran her nails across her lip and was hit by the sharp taste of hand sanitizer. She pulled her hand away. 'I wondered the same thing too.'

Seb picked up his drink. 'Maybe she didn't film it because the Japanese athlete didn't win . . .'

Hannah frowned. 'But she wouldn't have known that Jesse was going to win.'

'Maybe she doesn't like Haru, then.'

Hannah sighed. 'Maybe we're just reading too much into this.'

'No!' Maria objected. 'We need to be suspicious of everything.'

Seb reached over and grabbed the notebook. 'We should make a list of suspects.'

'Uh, sure.' Hannah hid the pen in her jacket pocket. 'I'll do that.'

'No, it's fine – I just need something to write with.' He turned to Hannah. 'Where's the pen?'

She pretended to look around. 'Do you not have it?'

'I don't think so . . .' He lifted up the notebook and shook his head. 'How have we now got two mysteries?'

Maria rummaged around in her belt bag. 'I have a pencil . . .'

She handed it to Seb and he opened up a fresh page in Hannah's notebook.

'Epic, thanks! This makes me feel really clever!'

Hannah itched in her seat as she watched Seb scribble down a wonky heading: *Suspects*.

'So, are we going to make the mean guard a suspect?' he asked.

Maria nodded. 'I think we should!'

As Seb wrote, Hannah reminded herself, *It's only pencil. You can rub it out and redo it later.*

'Anyone else?' he said.

Maria shrugged. 'Machi?'

'A director would steal a medal?' Hannah asked.

'Maybe.' Seb frowned. 'You think she did it?'

'Probably not,' said Maria. 'But you don't see Sherlock Holmes ignoring small clues.'

'These detectives seem to make things difficult for themselves. Too many suspects can't be helpful.' Seb passed the book back to Hannah.

'Sebastian,' said Maria, 'have you ever read a detective book?'

He shook his head.

'Seriously?'

'I only really read scripts. I'm reading *The Wizard of Oz* at the moment.'

Maria took a long slurp from her drink. 'Well, when this is all over, I've gotta lend you *The Ministry of Unladylike Activity*. It's one of my favourites.'

As they'd been chatting, another idea had popped into Hannah's head.

'We should search Machi's profile on Tokyo Games Social,' she said.

Seb smirked. 'Yes! Unlike Jesse, she seems like the type of person to document her entire life.'

Hannah opened up her phone and typed in Machi's

name. 'Cool, she has an account...'

'Good start,' said Maria.

Hannah tapped on Machi's profile. 'Okay... So she's uploaded all her previous work!'

'Probably so she can show off to all the famous movie-makers!' said Seb.

Hannah scrolled through the photos. 'She covered New York Fashion Week... and did a documentary about the queen's corgis!' She quickly scrolled back up to the top and followed Machi's account... *What a cool job*, Hannah thought to herself.

'Does it say where she was yesterday?' Maria asked, snapping Hannah back to the job at hand.

Hannah tapped through the sea of videos again. 'There's loads for today. A video inside the stadium... and another video inside the stadium... and another one...'

'Anything behind the scenes?' Maria asked.

Hannah picked up the pace. Eventually, she finished tapping through all the recent videos.

'There's a post from two days ago inside the velodrome, but nothing from yesterday.'

Seb jumped down from his stool and peered over Hannah's shoulder. 'Not even in a cafe? Or a car? Or a hotel?'

Hannah shook her head. 'Nothing.' She turned off her phone and pondered. 'It's like she didn't exist before.'

Maria pulled a smug face at Seb. 'See!' she said. 'I told you to investigate every clue!'

He rolled his eyes. 'Yeah, yeah.'

'I bet Machi didn't want anyone to know where she was.'

'What, because she was doing something dodgy?' Seb said.

Hannah agreed with Maria. 'Can you think of any other reason for why she wouldn't post anything?'

Seb paused for a moment, before shaking his head. 'Okay, then. Machi is our prime suspect.'

The friends were finishing their drinks at the sushi bar when Hannah's phone began to ring. She looked at the name of the caller.

'It's my dad!' She answered the call and whispered to the others, 'We should get back!'

On the other end of the phone she heard her dad say, 'Hello?'

'Hi, Dad!'

'Is everything okay? You've been gone for a while!'

'Yeah! Maria wanted to buy a T-shirt, but they didn't have her size.' She racked her brain. 'Then we joined in a game of catch with the volunteers!'

'Sounds like you've been busy!'

She laughed. 'We've had some food too!'

'Did you have enough money?'

'Maria's passes get us food and drinks.'

'Oh, sounds like you're all sorted ... but make sure you watch some of the shot put!'

As Hannah listened, she gestured to a sign indicating Block H.

'You're missing a real treat! Mereshko is unbelievable!'

Hannah and her friends hurried along the concourse.

'We'll be with you in two minutes!'

'Okay, see you soon!'

Hannah hung up the phone and pointed to a set of stairs. 'Up there!' The three of them rushed up to level two and towards Block H. They were met with a huge cluster of people, but Maria was soon weaving her way through. As Hannah forced her way into the huddle, she looked around to see what all the fuss was about.

'Look!' she yelled, coming to a halt as she took in the TV on the wall. 'It's an interview with Jesse!'

Maria and Seb joined Hannah amongst the swarm of fans and tiptoed to see the screen.

Seb craned his neck around a Dutch fan. 'I can't see!'

'Just listen, then!' said Hannah.

She weaved her way to the front of the crowd. The interview appeared to have been recorded after Jesse's race and before he received his medal.

The reporter asked, *'So, one-hundred-metre champion! How are you going to celebrate?'*

'We're actually pretty lucky!' Jesse told the interviewer. *'Some athletes have been invited to dinner tonight to celebrate the success of the American team!'*

'Is that for elite members?'

'No, no!' He shook his head. *'The dinner is for athletes who have represented the USA at three Games. It's a thank you to us veterans who have dedicated twelve years to the team.'*

The reporter smiled. *'Let's talk about that time. A world record! Did you expect that?'*

'My training had been going great, so I knew I could do it, but I didn't know if I was going to win. Haru is a great athlete, and I had no idea what time he was going to do!'

'You and Haru have such a great relationship. What is it that makes it so special?'

Jesse chuckled. *'We've been rivals since day one. We were constantly breaking each other's junior records. Haru used to practise his English with me too!'*

The interview ended and Hannah hurried back to the others.

'You heard that, right?' she asked them. 'About last night!'

'Yes!' Seb wagged his finger. 'We have to find out who was at that dinner.'

Maria gasped. 'Do you think Machi was filming it for her documentary?'

'Maybe!' said Hannah. 'But Sakura told us that there were loads of directors. Maybe they were all there?'

'We've gotta find out!' Maria insisted.

Seb pulled out his phone from his pocket. 'I know! I'll see if I can find a guest list online.'

Hannah watched as he typed in *Jesse Marks dinner* and scrolled through countless articles on the American and his missing medal. He tried searching for *Tokyo celebration dinner*, but there was nothing about it.

He shrugged. 'I guess they don't publish stuff like that...'

'That dinner was for the American team, wasn't it?' Hannah asked Maria.

She nodded. 'Oh... so we could look at the team's social posts, to see who was there?'

She gave Maria a wink and smiled. 'It's like you read my mind. You can search for them on my phone.'

The tannoy suddenly blared and the crowd erupted with cheers.

'Do you think your dad will give us more free time?' said Seb.

Hannah brought her hand to her mouth. 'Maria, do your passes get us into tours and stuff?'

'Of the venues, yeah.'

She turned Seb. 'I could tell my dad that we're on a tour . . .'

'It's the best lie we've got,' he said.

'We're not lying,' said Hannah. 'We're just going on an unofficial unguided tour.'

He laughed. 'If that's how you describe snooping around, then sure.'

'Look!' Maria showed them Hannah's phone. 'This post mentions the dinner was in the athletes' village!'

Hannah hugged Maria. 'Amazing, you found our first lead! Thank you!' She clutched the strap of her satchel. 'Right, I'll go and ask my dad if we can go for "a tour". I'll meet you at the gift shop from earlier!'

As Seb and Maria set off, Hannah dashed upstairs and crossed her fingers.

CHAPTER 9
NEXT STOP

Hannah ran into the gift shop, looking for Seb and Maria. She found them sitting around the Tokyo garden set. She fell back into a chair and grinned.

'Well, that was surprisingly easy.'

'So, your dad said yes?' Maria said.

'Yes!' She smiled. 'He was so engrossed in the shot put, he didn't mind at all.'

Seb fiddled with the patio parasol. 'How are we going to get to the athletes' village?'

'Well . . . I'm hoping there's a map of the whole Sportpark.' Hannah was looking around.

'But the athletes' village isn't in the Sportpark,' said Seb.

Hannah grabbed a map from the nearby stand and laid it down on the table. 'The athletes' village isn't, but the bus stops are.'

The three of them scanned the page.

'I can see the spectators' bus stop,' Maria said, turning her head to the side. 'I can't see an athlete stop, though.'

Seb shuffled closer to Hannah. 'Wow, it's so hard to see. The map is so busy!'

Hannah agreed. The left-hand side of the stadium was filled with labels and symbols . . . but the right-hand side of the stadium was completely empty.

'Hold on a second . . . Do you think that this isn't labelled because it's all athlete stuff?' Seb asked.

Maria smiled. 'That's gotta be right!'

'We haven't seen any athletes come or go,' said Seb, 'and they must be going somewhere.'

Maria studied the map again. 'How are we going to get to the other side of the stadium?'

Hannah noticed the main roads inside the Sportpark. One ran all the way down the middle, stopping off at each of the venues. 'That's the road for the spectators,' she pointed out. She then ran her finger along the other road, which encircled the entire park. 'But I don't know what this road is used for.'

'Wait a minute!' said Seb. 'I remember Katja Schultz, yesterday's long-jump winner, posted a video about waiting an hour for a bus.'

Hannah shook her head. 'But the buses were fine yesterday.'

'The athletes must have separate buses,' said Maria.

Hannah turned back to the map. 'I bet they use this other road! The buses pick them up on the opposite side of the stadium.'

Seb laughed. 'Phew, so *that's* why we don't see anyone!'

'Come on. Let's go!' Hannah stood up and returned the map to its stand. The three of them made their way to the exit. Stepping out into the daylight, Maria smiled as she looked back at the national stadium. 'This view never gets old.'

Hannah looked up at each level of the stadium, overhung with trees and shrubbery. The ledges they were perched on were specially designed to look like they were made from bamboo. A bird took off from one of the trees and she beamed. 'It's certainly very inventive.'

Hannah turned around and her eyes followed one of the blue-and-white fan buses as it made its way down the long, twisty path. She watched it reach the end of the Sportpark and join the main road.

The trio kept walking. After fifteen minutes, the other side of the stadium came into view.

'Quick, in here!' Seb pulled Hannah and Maria into a

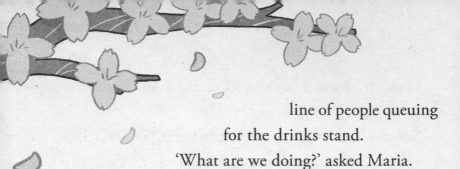

line of people queuing for the drinks stand.

'What are we doing?' asked Maria.

Seb peered round the stand. 'It looks like the athletes' bus stop is past that barrier.'

Hannah followed Seb's gaze and spotted a section fenced off by security guards. There was no way they were getting past them.

They kept on walking to the next venue along – the equestrian centre.

'Now what?' said Maria.

Hannah nodded towards a bench outside. 'Let's sit down for a minute.' She needed to update her notebook and this was as good a chance as any. As she pulled it out of her satchel, Maria squeaked.

'There's a bus coming – and it says ATHLETES' VILLAGE on the front!'

Hannah looked up, shoving her notebook back in her satchel. 'We need to follow it!'

'Follow it?!' said Maria.

'Yes! Follow it to the village!'

'How are we going to keep up?'

Hannah shrugged. 'No problem! If the traffic is busy . . . We just can't lose that coach before it leaves the Sportpark – we need to see which direction it goes.'

The trio leaped up and went hurtling down the middle of the park, weaving in and out of excited fans. Hannah glanced over her shoulder at the purple athletes' bus. They had a good head start – it was just pulling out of the stop.

'Are we going to make it?' Seb panted.

Behind her, Hannah saw the bus picking up speed. 'It'll be close!'

Maria ran ahead and cleared a path along the pavement for Seb and Hannah to follow.

They neared the aquatics centre.

'We're about halfway to the Sportpark gates,' said Hannah. But the bus wasn't far behind them. Hannah reckoned they'd reach the gate at exactly the same time. Breathing hard, she yelled to the others, 'It's . . . too . . . quick!'

Maria held out her hand. 'Seb, hold on!'

He grabbed her and flung out his other arm. Hannah stretched out her arm to complete the chain.

'I'm on!'

Maria gritted her teeth and tore down the pavement.

'It's going to be close!' she warned them.

As the friends hurled towards the exit, a group of volunteers leaped out of their way.

The bus roared behind them, and suddenly it was in front. They sprinted out of the gate just behind it, in time to see the purple bus turn left into a green-painted lane. It shot off into the distance, far faster than they could ever hope to run – even Maria.

Maria was still running, but slower now. 'Damn it!' she yelled.

'It's o-okay,' Hannah panted. 'Now w-we just follow the green lane! I read about the special lanes for athletes on the plane.'

Maria strode off quickly, not even out of breath, Hannah and Seb shuffling behind.

Hannah shook her head and smiled. Next stop, the athletes' village!

Hannah gasped when she finally caught her first glimpse of the athletes' village. They'd been walking for miles, or so it had seemed, and her feet were aching, but now she forgot all about them.

Even from a distance, it looked absolutely enormous. Its tall, white apartment blocks towered over the rest of the neighbourhood. Outside each apartment, a flag was draped over the balcony.

'That's cool!' she said, recognizing a yellow-blue-and-red-striped flag and a black-red-and-green one. 'Colombia and Kenya are sharing that level!'

Seb peered over her shoulder. 'How do you know? Can you tell from the flags?'

'You could say they're my hidden talent. My mum

used to test me on them all the time!'

'What's the flag next to Great Britain, then?'

Hannah realized the largest teams like Great Britain had an entire block to themselves. Next door was another block draped with dark blue flags with little white stars, though the building itself was wrapped in bright green-and-gold banners.

'That's easy!' she said. 'Australia!'

Maria, with seemingly endless energy, zoomed ahead of them. 'I've seen so many photos of the village, but it's way more awesome in real life!'

Hannah smiled. 'It's like their own little corner of the world.'

'I've heard the athletes call it a bubble,' Maria said, 'because it isn't like anywhere they've ever been before.'

'It's impossible to think there would be a thief in there,' Hannah said. 'It's all too perfect!'

'If the medal was stolen at the dinner, then a guest could've done it,' Seb said.

Hannah shrugged. 'Or someone else from the outside.'

'If we get into the village, then we can ask Jesse himself,' Maria said. 'You know – where he went, the last place he saw the medal . . . that kinda stuff.' She jumped up and down. 'We're actually going to meet him!'

'That's a good point!' said Hannah. 'Is he competing today?'

'Yeah, he is, but his two-hundred-metre final isn't until the evening.'

'Okay, so when we're inside,' Hannah said, 'we need to find Jesse first.'

'Obviously! So we don't miss him,' Seb joked.

'*And* because he can tell us whether he had his medal at the dinner. That's really important to our investigation.'

Maria kicked a pebble along the pavement. 'Yeah – if he didn't, then we know it was stolen before.'

Seb nodded. 'Then it would have to be someone on the inside. An inside job.'

'Okay, but don't get too carried away.' Hannah opened up her satchel. 'We'll see what Jesse has to say. I just hope we're the first people to talk to him – besides the police. Who knows how many others are trying to find the medal and get the reward.'

She took out her notebook and started a fresh page entitled *Village Clues*. As she returned the book to her bag, Seb teased, 'Keep our options open . . .'

Hannah buckled up her satchel. 'It's the number one rule!'

She looked up to see the village in all its glory, bearing down on the trio.

'Okay.' Hannah took a deep breath. 'Now we just need to get in.'

CHAPTER 10
SPRING FRESH

Hannah, Seb and Maria peered round the house on the corner of the street.

About fifty metres away was the checkpoint for the athletes' village. To Hannah, it seemed to go on for miles. The checks began with a line of heavily armed security guards. Behind them was a huge metal gate and a bus-sized airport scanner. Past that was where the buses dropped off the athletes at the village bus stop.

'I have a feeling this isn't going to be easy.' Seb squeezed his head between the girls' shoulders.

'It's going to be impossible,' Maria groaned.

Hannah crouched down and surveyed the queue of vehicles waiting at the checkpoint. A purple athlete bus, a lorry, another athlete bus, a yellow bus, another lorry, and, finally, another purple athlete bus.

She whispered to the others, 'It looks like only vehicles can get in – there's no one on foot.'

Maria looked down at her and shrugged. 'So . . . ?'

'We have to get into one!' Hannah pointed to the queue, which was almost around the corner.

Seb poked his head through again. 'We're not going to get on a bus without accreditation.' He looked at his pastel shirt and shorts combo. 'Even if we did, we're not going to get very far dressed like this!'

Hannah glanced down at the forties blouse and culottes she'd carefully curated that morning. 'You're right.' She raised her head to watch the athletes piling off at the bus stop. 'We need to be in kit to get on a bus.'

Maria dipped back behind the wall. 'Where on earth are we going to find team kit?'

All three slumped down against the wall, out of ideas, watching a van turn off the main road and join the queue for the village.

Seb smiled. 'Have you noticed how the cars here are all shaped like perfect boxes?'

'That can't be very aerodynamic!' Hannah laughed, thinking of her favourite F1 cars.

Seb and Maria carried on chatting while she stared at the cartoon on the back of the van. A little washing machine overflowing with soap suds. One of the double doors flapped slightly as it moved.

'Oi! You two!' She nudged Seb to get his attention. 'Look at that laundry van!'

From the other side of him, Maria leaned forward. 'What about it?'

Hannah got to her feet. 'Maybe it can get us into the village. It looks like the back door's unlocked.'

Standing up, Seb peered around the corner again. 'How do we make sure the guards don't see us?'

Hannah placed her hand on his shoulder. 'Because, my friend, you have the most important job.'

'Which is . . . ?'

'Distracting the driver.'

Seb gulped. 'Right . . . because I can act.'

Maria removed her pin badge from her pass and handed it to Seb. 'Make yourself look like a pin enthusiast.'

Hannah quickly gave him hers too. 'A driver would go in and out of the village a lot,' she said, 'so they probably have pins.'

Seb nodded.

'Oh, and pretend that you live near here,' Hannah added. 'That your dad just got a job in Tokyo.'

'I'm not sure that will come up in conversation?'

he said, laughing.

Hannah gave him one last instruction. 'Then, as soon as you've finished chatting, jump into the back with us. We'll leave the door open for you.'

'Right.'

'Go!' hissed Hannah, sending him off on his mission.

As he approached the van, Hannah turned to Maria.

'Okay, once the driver is distracted, we need to open the back of the van and climb inside.'

'What if we get caught?' Maria squeaked.

Hannah watched Seb head for the driver's door. 'We won't...' She smiled. 'It's perfect, actually. The driver is parked just after the zebra crossing.'

Maria nudged her glasses up her nose. 'So there's less distance to walk?'

Hannah pointed to the queue of traffic. 'The guards on the left can't see the other side of the road because the buses are in the way.'

'Ah, okay...'

'Do you get it now?'

Maria shook her head. 'Nah, not really.'

Hannah smiled. 'If we look like we're crossing the road, the guards won't know if we don't make it to the other side.'

'Oh, I get you – so they won't know we've climbed into the van!'

They both watched as the driver wound the window down and began to speak to Seb. With a sweet smile, Seb showed off the badges on his collar.

Maria whispered. 'Do we go now?'

Hannah held out her hand. 'Just a second...'

The driver leaned out of the window to take a closer look at Seb's pins.

'Amazing!' Hannah beamed. 'It's actually working!'

The driver began unfastening a badge from her own pass. Hannah stood up straight.

'Now!'

The girls set off along the zebra crossing. Out of the corner of her eye, Hannah monitored the driver, making sure she was still distracted.

Reaching the back of the van, Hannah grabbed the loose door, had a quick check that no one was looking and swung it open, jumping inside. As Maria joined her, they both crawled over a stack of detergent and squashed themselves behind a large laundry basket at the front.

It was a squeeze, but there was just enough space. The smell of freshly washed clothes was overpowering in such a small space. She did her best to fight a cough in the back of her throat. She covered her face with her sleeve and the two of them listened, waiting for Seb.

'Well, thank you so much!' Seb said to the driver in full 'diplomat mode'.

'No, thank you!'

The driver sounded English, thought Hannah. That was useful!

'My dad will love this!' Seb said. 'We just moved here and I wanted to get him something nice.'

Ha, he did use my backstory! thought Hannah.

'Have a nice day!' Seb said.

Hannah pressed an ear to the front panel of the van and heard the driver turning on the radio. She waited for Seb to appear at the door they'd left slightly ajar, but he was nowhere to be seen.

The engine began to rumble and Maria whispered, 'Where is he?'

Hannah climbed on to a box of detergent and tried to peer around one of the rear doors. She'd just managed to poke her head over the top when the box slipped from beneath her and she fell back into the van.

'Hey!' hissed a voice. Seb's face appeared at the door at last. '*Make room!*' he mouthed, lifting his foot.

But at that moment, the van started moving. Seb lost

his footing, tripped and stumbled to the ground.

Maria fumbled her way to the back of the van and stretched out her arm. 'Hold on!'

Hannah wedged herself between boxes and grabbed Maria's other hand to help her balance, as Seb picked himself up and chased after them.

Hannah whispered, 'Be careful! The driver might hear us!'

The van began to speed up and Hannah wondered how close they were to the guards. Would Seb be seen?

Seb broke into a run.

Hannah heard voices shouting to each other, followed by the stamping of boots.

Maria shuffled closer to the edge, until she was almost hanging out of the van.

'Come on!' Maria whispered.

Hannah could see Seb just about touching Maria's fingers.

'I'm . . . trying . . .' he panted.

Hannah recognized that one of the voices was now shouting in English.

'You! Stop!'

She felt Maria slipping from her sweaty palm. 'Oh no, oh no, oh no . . .'

Then all of a sudden she felt herself flying to the front of the van as it screeched to a halt.

As Hannah fell to the floor, boxes cascaded down on top of her. She pushed away the detergent to see Seb shooting through the van door. He brought Maria down with a crash and winced. 'Ow! My arm!'

Maria scraped her leg from under him. '*Your* arm?' She rolled her eyes. 'What about my leg?'

Hannah put her fingers to her lips. 'Keep quiet and close that door!'

Maria quickly sat up while Seb pulled the handle with his uninjured arm.

Hannah continued to listen out for the guards, pressing her ear to the side of the van. She heard someone questioning the driver in English. She ushered her friends closer and they eavesdropped together.

'. . . and you won't drive that fast again?'

'No, I won't. I'm sorry.'

'Thank you. You may continue.'

The van moved forward and a gate clattered open.

'I think we're in the village!' Hannah whispered.

Seb held up his hand and grinned. 'High-fives all round!'

Hannah returned the high-five. 'What took you so long to get in the van? I thought the guards had spotted you and that's why the van stopped!'

Seb shrugged. 'I needed to attach my new badge.'

'Oh!' she mocked. 'You needed to attach your badge!'

The van trundled through the village and Maria turned to Hannah.

'So, next question: how do we get out without anyone seeing us?'

Hannah looked around the van. 'I reckon we hide at the back when they stop. If they take stuff out, maybe there will be a chance for us to slip out once they're gone.' She bit her nails. She knew it wasn't the greatest idea, but it was better than nothing.

Hannah heard a gate open up ahead.

The sound of footsteps hitting concrete and metal carts clattering together echoed outside. The trio moved to the back of the van, as far from the doors as they could, and crouched down amongst the boxes.

Hannah felt the van moving backwards and assumed the driver was parking. The engine turned off and she heard people approaching. Outside she heard a hatch slide open followed by the van doors. The people outside were speaking in Japanese as they reached into the van for the basket next to the doors. She peeped over the boxes, holding her breath, and recognized a flash of blue uniform.

The basket was pulled out and the sound of voices moved further away. Hannah let out a sigh. 'Quick, let's get out!' she hissed, leaping over the laundry things as quietly as she could and slipping through the van door.

She slung her satchel over her shoulder and scanned the room as Seb and Maria joined her. It was grey, concrete and dark. She spotted a gap between a row of tumble dryers and the wall.

'Behind here!'

They crammed themselves into the space in case anyone returned. There was a strong smell of something that Hannah guessed had a name like *Spring Fresh* or *Summer Breeze*. Whatever it was, it was nicer than the suffocating detergent in the van.

Hannah was glad that Seb and Maria were doing all the talking. She heard more footsteps and some Japanese chatter and something that sounded like boxes being dropped on to the ground. Hannah tiptoed to peek over the industrial washing machine and saw three people leaving the laundry room, laughing. Maria took a sharp breath and flapped her hands.

'She's going to sneeze!' Seb whispered.

Hannah shoved her hand over Maria's mouth to muffle the noise.

'Achoo!'

The group of people fell quiet and one of them pushed the door back open. Hannah could hear him pacing around the room as he shouted something to his friends. Hannah ducked as low as she could, but she heard his footsteps approaching and mouthed to the others, *'He's coming!'*

They shuffled in closer and waited for a stern telling-off, at the least. How would they explain this? The volunteer rapped his fingers on the metal and Hannah's throat squeezed.

'There you are . . .'

She heard something being swept away from the top of the washing machine. 'I thought I'd lost this jacket!'

Hannah sagged with relief, listened to his footsteps as he left the room, and only then let out an enormous sigh. She stole a glance over the machine and gestured to the others. 'He's gone.'

Seb got to his feet shakily. 'I thought that was it!' he squeaked.

Maria shook her head. 'I still don't know how we're going to sneak around here. There are probably workers everywhere!'

'We need to find disguises,' Hannah said.

Seb laughed. 'Well, you've come to the right place! There's kit everywhere!' He pointed to a nearby countertop.

Hannah surveyed the team kit stacked in piles. It was all neatly organized into white mesh bags with different-coloured ribbons. She darted over to the tables and smiled.

'It looks so cool!' She hesitated. 'We can't take it, can we?'

'No.' Maria stepped forward. 'But you also can't steal a gold medal.'

Hannah looked at their ticket to getting out of there and continuing their investigation, sprawled all over the counter.

'We can give them back as soon as we're done, right?'

Maria nodded. 'Of course.'

'Plus, the athletes must get loads of kit,' said Seb. 'They might not even notice that it's missing.'

Hannah turned to Maria. 'Which do you think we should wear?'

'You're asking me?'

'You're the athlete.'

'But I've never investigated a medal thief!'

Hannah surveyed the counter and the labels on the ribbons. There was every country she could ever think of, from North Macedonia to South Korea.

'We need to pick an English-speaking team, otherwise our disguises won't get us far.'

Seb rummaged around and collected a couple of bags from the pile. 'I can't see a Great Britain pile. But we've got Australia or the United States.' He turned to Hannah. 'How's your Aussie accent?'

She pulled a face. 'Awful. Plus Maria actually has an American accent.'

'Ayy! You don't think I do too?' Seb said, in what wasn't a bad New Yorker accent, Hannah guessed.

Hannah laughed. 'That was brilliant!'

Maria gave him a playful punch. 'Not bad, kid.'

'Okay, then . . .' Hannah took the bag of American kit. 'Let's hope this fits.' She quickly unzipped the bag and started to size up the T-shirts, jackets and trousers. 'Yes, we made the right choice,' Hannah announced.

'I know!' Maria ducked behind the row of dryers to get changed. 'The US kit is awesome this year.'

'There is that . . .' said Hannah. 'And it'll be much easier to get into their apartment block, too.'

CHAPTER 11
UNDERCOVER

Suited up in her American team kit, Hannah poked her head round the door.

'It looks empty out here,' she told the others. Behind her, Maria was studying a noticeboard on the laundry-room wall.

'I know him!'

'Who?' Hannah dipped back inside.

Maria pointed to a lanyard. 'Cam Dyke. The guy on this accreditation! He was on our World Junior Team last year.'

Seb flicked through the other lanyards. 'There are a few here.'

'What do you think they're doing up there?' asked Hannah.

Maria pushed her glasses up her nose. 'Lost and found?'

Hannah looked for a sign, but all the writing was in Japanese.

Seb took Cam's lanyard off the hook. 'They probably found their way into the laundry bags by accident.' He hung it around his neck. 'We look kind of similar, don't you think?'

Hannah bit her nails. 'Should we really be stealing another athlete's pass?'

Seb straightened up and laughed. 'No worries, I'll return it when we're done! Besides, these athletes have probably got new ones by now. It's just some card and plastic.' He continued flicking through the others on the hook. 'Hey, this girl even looks a little like you, Hannah!'

Hannah took the accreditation from Seb. The girl in the photo did have the same high forehead, fair hair and bright blue eyes. Hannah read aloud, 'Anastasia Shevchenko.'

Maria pulled another lanyard from the noticeboard and Hannah saw a picture of a girl with curly brown hair. 'Nina Ramone. That will have to do!'

Having crammed her clothes into her satchel, Hannah was pretty pleased with her disguise.

At least if they got caught now, they'd be mistaken for athletes. Maybe they'd even be escorted back to the US apartment block.

'So, what sport do we do?' asked Seb. 'We need to have our story straight if it comes up in conversation.'

Maria pushed up her glasses. 'That's a good point . . . Gymnasts are pretty young. We could do that?'

He shrugged. 'I can be a gymnast.'

Oh god . . . Hannah had a sudden thought – how could *she* be a gymnast with one arm? How could she compete at the Games with one arm? The Para Games wasn't until next month. Surely people would question why she was here now. With her disability, they wouldn't believe that she was an athlete – and she was way too young to be a coach or physio.

She knew what she had to do, and it didn't feel good.

'Hold on . . . I need to cover up . . .'

Even though it was hot, she pulled the USA jacket out of her satchel.

'Cover wha—?' Seb stopped abruptly 'Oh, yeah . . . sorry. The Para Games is a separate competition, isn't it?'

Maria gave Hannah a sympathetic smile. 'It sucks you gotta do that.'

Hannah forced a smile and stuck her sticky, sweaty

arm through a sleeve. 'It's okay. It just reminds me of when my mum would take me out.' She fiddled with the zip and fastened the jacket. 'In some places, I was stared at so much. It made me wear long sleeves so people wouldn't notice that I only had one arm.'

She made her way to the door and her friends walked behind her.

'It's weird,' said Seb, 'because I don't think about it. Wait . . . that's not mean, is it?'

Hannah smiled. 'Not at all. There are more important things to think about.' She chuckled. 'What I have to say is much more interesting.'

'That's true!' he said.

Through the door, Hannah spotted another laundry van parking up. 'Now, let's get out of here!'

The trio rushed out and found themselves walking through what looked like a huge concrete basement.

'Is this a car park?' asked Maria.

'I don't know.' Seb shrugged. 'Though we must be underground. There aren't any windows.'

Hannah looked around. Wherever they were, it was pretty empty. Every now and then, a buggy drove past, a van parked up or an athlete passed by. 'Well, we need to find a way out somewhere!'

'What's in there?' Maria asked, pointing to a dark corridor up ahead. Hannah took a step closer and saw light shining in from the top of a long ramp.

'Looks like a way out of here.' Hannah said hopefully.

They rushed through and climbed the ramp, Maria streaking ahead.

Already at the top, Maria was bathed in light from a glass door. 'We're about to see what the athletes' village looks like. Come on!'

Now Hannah broke into a run, and soon all three were pushing a door open into the sunshine. She looked up and saw a balcony draped in South African flags, where an athlete lounged on a beanbag. Athletes of all nations walked up and down the pavements. Buses drove slowly along sweeping roads. Each block of flats shared an island with its neighbours, and the roads were like the sea. The friends walked past an enormous building with the words FOOD HALL across the front.

'An entire building of food!' Seb gawped. 'It's two-storey!'

'Are you always thinking about food?' Maria joked.

He shrugged. 'Maybe about eighty per cent of the time?'

'Not now!' Hannah said. 'We need to spend one hundred per cent of our time looking for Jesse!'

Finally they spotted a block draped in American flags and Maria sped up.

'Right,' said Maria. 'Let's find him!'

They made their way along the path. Each American they passed shot them a smile. Hannah smiled but tried not to make eye contact, just in case they stopped to talk and saw their accreditation. If anyone knew Anastasia, Nina or Cam, they'd be quickly exposed as imposters!

Maria beamed. "This is so cool!'

Hannah fetched her camera from her satchel. 'Quick photo before we go inside.'

She extended her arm and turned the camera towards them. Seb and Maria huddled in closer and grinned.

'Hey!' a voice interrupted. A tall girl in French kit held out her hand. 'I can take that for you.'

Hannah waited for Maria and Seb to say thank you so she didn't have to risk her American accent.

The girl crouched down and angled the camera. 'Ready?'

Hannah stood between Maria and Seb and nodded.

The camera clicked.

'You look great!' the girl said, smiling.

Hannah took the camera back and gave Maria a nudge, hoping that it would prompt her to ask about Jesse's apartment.

Maria took the hint and smiled nervously. 'Do you know which apartment Jesse Marks is staying in?' she asked.

The girl craned her neck and looked up at the American block. 'Do *I* know? Why, I have no idea!' She turned to the others. 'Surely someone on your team knows?'

'Yeah, you're right.' Maria forced a smile. 'Sorry.'

The athlete took another look at the block. 'My friend said the American relay team is sharing a flat, but that's all I know. He's in the team, I think?'

'Ah, that helps a bit,' Maria said. 'Thank you.'

'Sorry I don't know any more.' She waved goodbye. 'I'll see you around.'

The three of them waved back.

As the girl set off down the path, Maria turned to face the US block. 'Well,' she said. 'He could be in any one of those.'

Hannah pulled her phone from her pocket. 'I think I know which one . . .'

'You do?' said Seb.

'I might.'

The friends made their way towards the US block and Hannah explained her idea. 'I think my fact file said that Aaron Wykoff is on the relay team.' She turned around. 'Maria, is that right?'

'Yeah.'

'I remember he posted a behind-the-scenes video on the Tokyo Social app.'

'Oh, I saw that too,' Seb said. 'Could you see which apartment he was in? I can't remember.'

Hannah pictured the front door in her head. 'It was . . . 4C!'

Seb took her hand and began to skip down the path. 'Let's go!' he cried, as his lanyard clinked against his jacket. He grabbed Maria's hand too and grinned. 'Aw, look at us. Best friends!'

Hannah smiled. She wasn't sure she'd ever made friends so quickly, but it felt good – even if they were nowhere near solving the Gold Medal Mystery.

They walked through a little garden outside the American block, and Hannah hurried them past a group of athletes sunning themselves on deckchairs.

'Don't let any US athletes get a good look at you,' she said. 'They might work out that we're imposters.'

The trio arrived outside the entrance to the apartment block and Hannah put her accreditation under a metal scanner at the porch. She suddenly thought – would it work? Maybe it would have been cancelled. But an animated figure on the screen above gave her a thumbs up and the automatic door slid open.

'*Open Sesame!*' sang Maria.

They wandered inside and the door slid shut behind them.

Hannah walked past the front desk and the ground floor opened up into a big living area filled with TVs, beanbags, sofas and fridges.

'Woah!' Maria gasped. 'This is—'

'Epic.' Seb stared at one of the TVs broadcasting the swimming. 'Totally epic!'

There was a big commotion over in the corner, where about twenty athletes were all squashed on to one couch.

'Aw, they're watching the heats together.' Maria was listening to the commentators announcing the swimmers. 'Ooh, the guy in lane four is good. He's won the two-hundred-metre medley three times in a row!'

Hannah ushered her over to the other side of the room. 'I think the lifts are down this corridor.'

'How do you know that?' Seb asked.

There was a loud *ding* in the distance, followed by the muffled sound of opening doors.

'You know, that could just be it,' Maria joked.

It wasn't long before they found their way inside a lift and Maria began pressing buttons.

'Floor four?' She scanned her finger over the options –

LG, G, M, I, 2, 3, 4, 5, 6, 7, 8 – and turned to the others. 'What on earth is M?'

Hannah pressed the four button and let the doors shut before anyone else tried to hitch a ride. 'M is for MEZZANINE. It's basically level one and a half.'

The lift started to move and Maria laughed. 'That's so confusing.'

'Hey, I'm just glad we're not going as high as the Skytree!' said Seb, shuddering. The levels slowly climbed. 'So, what are we going to say when Jesse answers the door?'

'We could pretend to be athletes congratulating him,' said Hannah, 'and then ask some casual questions. We just need to make sure we keep our accreditation hidden, in case he knows Cam, Nina or Anastasia.'

The lift doors opened and they stepped out into the corridor.

Hannah pointed straight ahead. 'There it is . . . flat 4C.'

Maria turned to the others, her brown eyes alight. 'Can I knock on the door? It's literally my biggest wish ever to speak to Jesse! I know

129

we met him yesterday – but this is different . . .'

'I'd be a total monster if I said no,' Hannah replied.

Seb nodded. 'It's definitely your turn.'

'Awesome, thanks!' She skipped over to the door.

Hannah followed and waited for Maria to knock.

She stood staring at the number on the door.

'Feeling a bit nervous?' Seb whispered.

Maria sighed. 'Yeah, I just can't help feeling I'm gonna mess it up.'

'You won't mess it up!' he said. 'We're here to congratulate Jesse and ask him all about winning gold. In fact, you're the perfect person to do it, because you're a true superfan!'

'Yeah!' Maria smiled, pushing up her glasses. 'I'll just be myself.'

She raised her hand and knocked three times.

Hannah could hear a few voices from inside the apartment, and someone drawing closer until they answered the door.

'Hello?'

Hannah recognized the face from Aaron Wykoff's post. Twinkling hazel eyes, dark brown locs and a perfect white smile. This was Marcus Draper.

Maria gave a sheepish smile. 'Hi, we were kinda wondering whether we could speak with Jesse.'

Marcus's perfect smile turned to a scowl. 'Yeah?' he snarled. 'Well, he's not in.'

He began to close the door.

'Wait!' Seb shouted.

Marcus reluctantly pulled the door ajar and looked through the gap. 'Yeah?'

'Could you tell Jesse that we were here?' Seb said in his New Yorker accent.

Hannah pulled her notebook from her bag. 'You can have my number to pass on to Jesse . . . ?' She quickly tore out a page and scribbled it down.

'And mine!' Seb, said.

Hannah handed the piece of paper with both their numbers over to Marcus.

He shook his head. 'If you want Jesse, you can find him online.'

'But he doesn't have—' Seb started to say.

It was too late. Marcus screwed the page into a ball and slammed the door shut.

Hannah pressed her ear against it. As he walked away, she heard his words echo through the hall. 'Why does everybody love him? If only they knew what he was really like.'

CHAPTER 12
M

Hannah left Marcus's apartment and rushed over to the others. They held the lift doors open and she ran inside.

She waited for the lift to start moving. 'I listened to Marcus through the door and he said something really odd.'

'I'm guessing he didn't have anything nice to say about us?' Maria snarled.

'I don't think it was us he had the problem with.'

'What did he say?' asked Seb.

'"Why does everybody love him? If only they knew what he was really like,"' Hannah repeated.

'Wow.' Maria shook her head. 'He must hate Jesse.'

'Or there is something else we don't know about him,' said Seb.

Maria raised an eyebrow. 'Like what?'

'I don't know.' He shrugged. 'Maybe he's not as nice as everyone thinks he is . . .'

'No way!' Maria protested. 'You can't say that!'

'*Level one*,' said the lift announcement.

They stopped and the doors slid open to let an athlete inside.

Hannah quickly read his accreditation: Harvey Simpson. She didn't recognize the name, but she didn't know if Harvey Simpson knew Anastasia Shevchenko. She gifted him a smile and turned to face the others, while making sure her loose jacket sleeve didn't look obvious.

Maria rolled her eyes at Seb, probably still angry about his accusation. Hannah caught her gaze and gestured towards Harvey. '*Who's that?*' she mouthed.

Maria shrugged and tucked her accreditation into her jacket. The others quickly copied and waited for the awkward journey to end.

A few seconds later the lift reached the ground floor and Hannah rushed out, looking for somewhere they'd be alone. She found a small door labelled QUIET ROOM further along the corridor and led Seb and Maria inside, closing the door and sitting down at one of the desks.

Seb flopped down on to a beanbag. 'So much for finding Jesse!'

Hannah untucked her accreditation. 'Well, hiding these was a good idea. We don't want the real Anastasia, Nina and Cam to see us . . . or their friends.'

'Imagine if they did!' Maria stole a glance at the window. 'We could be caught any second.'

'Which is why we should be quick.' Hannah turned to Maria. 'Do you have any idea why Marcus hates Jesse so much?'

'They're both sprinters, but Marcus focuses on the two hundred metres now, I think.'

'I'll make some notes.' Hannah opened up her bag. 'Seb, can you check the results, please? Find out how Marcus has been performing?'

She turned to Maria, who gave her a salute.

'And for me, ma'am?'

'Ha ha.' Hannah rolled her eyes, passing her phone to Maria. 'Search for anything about Marcus's career . . . Oh, and his relationship with Jesse.'

Seb and Maria got to work while Hannah flicked to her list of suspects. Under Machi's name, she wrote *Marcus Draper?* She was starting a new page for Marcus, just as Seb leaned forward to read an article aloud.

'*Yesterday saw Draper in action for the first time this Games, with a one-hundred-metre semi-final sprint that was*

134

good enough for twelfth – well off the pace of the finalists.'

Hannah scribbled down *100 metres = twelfth.*

'It says here that he held the longstanding American record for the one hundred metres until four years ago,' Maria added, 'when Jesse broke it on his way to claiming his first Games gold.' She paused. 'Oh yeah, I remember that.'

'It's interesting,' said Hannah.

'Do you think he's jealous of Jesse?' Seb asked, looking up from his phone.

Maria read a little further down. 'I was right – it says here that Marcus now focuses on the two hundred metres.'

Despite Marcus's frosty façade, Hannah felt an inkling of pity for him. 'Maybe he switched to the two hundred metres so people would stop comparing him to Jesse.'

'You're probably right.' Seb nodded. 'Who wants to be known as "Jesse's teammate"?'

Hannah heard the cheers of the group on the sofa in the foyer. She turned to the window and watched them jumping up and down. 'Aw.'

Maria smiled. 'I bet they're cheering on Tiffany Wilde. It's her last-ever race today. I need to remember to watch the highlights later!'

'Why can't Marcus be as supportive as them?' said Seb.

'Because he's jealous of the attention?' Hannah suggested.

'Jealous enough to steal Jesse's medal?' he joked.

The room fell quiet.

The three of them turned to one another, until Maria broke the silence.

'You really think so?'

'We can't rule him out,' said Hannah. 'I've written his name down.'

'I guess there's no harm in that,' said Seb.

'It *is* the perfect crime,' she said.

'It is?' Maria blinked.

'Well, yeah. He's got access to Jesse's room, and it's not like Jesse's going to search through his flatmate's belongings for his medal. Marcus could keep the medal in his pocket if he liked!'

'Jeez.' Maria shook her head. 'Hiding the medal right under Jesse's nose.'

Seb jumped to his feet. 'We could try to search the flat?'

'How would we do that . . . ?' Hannah said.

'We could . . . uh . . .'

'Wait, I know!' said Hannah.

'Good!' He laughed. 'Because I have nothing.'

'Seeing as Marcus wants the attention, Maria can ask him for an interview.'

Maria frowned. 'But he thinks I'm an athlete.'

'But you could still have a podcast? Or a YouTube channel?'

'Won't he only be interested in TV interviews?'

'Not necessarily...' said Seb. 'Depends how many subscribers you have.'

Maria nudged her glasses up. 'I'm not sure...'

'And while he's distracted,' Hannah continued, 'Seb can search the flat and I'll keep lookout.'

'Why am I searching it?' Seb whined.

'Because if he sees you, you can put on an American accent.'

'And that will stop him from being suspicious?'

Hannah placed a hand on his shoulder. 'I'm sorry, but he'll be more suspicious of an English accent – or a terrible American one.'

He nodded. 'Okay, I'll do it.'

They turned to Maria, eyes wide.

She breathed out loudly. 'Jeez, all right. Anything for Jesse, I guess.'

Hannah slotted her notebook back in her satchel, secretly relieved that she didn't have to sneak around the flat. She got up from her seat and peered out of the door. She saw a swarm of coaches pile into the lifts and turned to the others.

'We'll have to take the stairs back up. The lifts are way too busy. It's too risky – we might get found out.'

Maria poked her head round the door and pointed to the stairwell past the lift. 'We just have to keep our heads down.'

She led the three of them to the stairs, weaving in and out of the coaches. 'Up here,' she whispered, darting through a small gap in the wall and once more taking the steps two at a time.

'She's so quick!' Hannah panted.

Behind her, Seb plodded along. 'Tell her I'm not a stunt actor and I don't do action movies.'

Hannah slowed down to walk alongside Seb. As they reached the next set of stairs, she told him, 'Even though this is the most stressful thing I've ever done, it's kind of fun. I just hope my dad isn't wondering where we are.'

He laughed. 'What's stressful? Walking up four flights of stairs?'

'You know I mean the investigation! I hate that we haven't found anything. And I don't know if my dad is going to let me go off with you both every day, especially if he finds out I left the stadium. Today might be our only chance to find the medal!'

'Be optimistic,' said Seb. 'We could have plenty of time!'

The two of them turned the last corner.

'But what if we don't! And maybe someone else will find the medal first. There's a big reward after all. We might put all this work in but still fail!'

He nodded. 'We might.'

'And you're happy with that?'

Seb shrugged. 'I'm happy knowing I tried my best and made friends along the way.'

'We are very different!' Hannah chuckled.

'You could be more positive, you know?'

At the top of the stairs, Maria waved. 'Hey! We haven't got all day!'

'You see!' said Hannah. 'Maria gets it!'

Seb shook his head. 'Maria's just excited – and you should be too!' He sprinted the last few steps to the top. 'Come on!'

Hannah ran after him and joined them both at the top.

Maria rolled her eyes. 'I'm definitely not signing you up for the ten thousand metres.'

They headed towards Marcus's flat. 'I'd like to see *you* do it!' Seb joked.

'Trust me, no one wants to see that!' Maria shook her head.

Hannah brought them together into a huddle well away from the apartment door. 'Okay, so here's the plan. Seb and I go and hide. Maria knocks on the door. When she goes inside, she leaves it ajar. Cool so far?'

The others nodded.

'Maria, try to get Marcus out on the balcony to interview him, so that Seb can sneak in. And make sure you give Seb a warning by saying, "This is my last question," so that Seb can get out before you come back inside. Hopefully that should give him enough time.' She stood up straight. 'Sounds good?'

They nodded again and Seb saluted. 'Yes, ma'am.'

'Cool. Now Seb and I need to find somewhere to hide.'

Hannah looked around and spotted a scooter shed by the lift. 'That should work.'

Seb ran over and stuck his head inside. 'It's definitely big enough.'

While he ducked inside, Hannah turned to Maria. 'Are you okay with it all?'

She took a deep breath. 'Yeah. I just gotta be myself. I'm an athlete and I'm a fan.'

'You've got this.'

She gave Maria a thumbs up and rushed to join Seb.

Hannah tucked herself between a scooter and the wall, and she and Seb pressed their ears to the door to listen out.

Maria knocked on the apartment. There was a pause, then—

'Hey, Marcus!' she said.

'Ugh. What do you want?'

'Wait! Before you close the door!'

Silence.

'Thank you,' Maria sighed.

'I said, what do you want?'

'I want an interview with you.'

'Oh, really?'

'Yeah! I have my own YouTube channel where I interview other athletes who made it at a young age.'

'Oh, you do?'

Hannah could sense the sarcasm lacing his voice.

'Yeah!' Maria replied.

'Well, it seems like you came here looking for Jesse, but when you couldn't find him, you settled for me.'

'No! Not at all!'

'Well, go find somebody else,' Marcus snarled. 'I'm no one's second best.'

The door slammed shut.

'Ugh!' Hannah kicked one of the scooters and a pain shot through her foot. 'Ow!' She gritted her teeth. 'Now I have two problems.'

She hobbled out of the scooter shed after Seb.

'What happened to you?' Maria said, nodding at Hannah's foot.

'I'm just so annoyed. You did a good job and he still didn't want to talk!'

Maria gave a half-hearted smile. 'Thanks, Hannah.'

Seb made his way over to the lift. 'We may not have found the medal, but he's got to be another suspect.'

The pain started to ease from Hannah's foot and she tried to see the funny side. 'It's like Investigation "M". Marks's medal stolen by Machi or Marcus.'

'Who do you think did it?' asked Maria.

Seb smiled. 'Well, your name begins with M – maybe it's you!'

'Watch it!'

'Whoever did it,' said Hannah, 'we need to find them soon.' The lift doors opened and the three of them stepped inside, relieved it was empty. 'And we really need to find Jesse!'

Seb pressed the button for the ground floor. 'Where do we go next?'

'I'm hoping Maria has an idea.'

'Me?' she said.

'Yeah, you're an athlete. How do you prepare for a final?'

'I normally grab some lunch and then have a nap beforehand.'

'You sleep before competing?'

'Five hours before, yeah. It's not like I'm still napping five minutes before the start!'

'In that case, maybe Jesse's in the food hall?' Hannah suggested.

Maria checked her watch. 'His final isn't for another six hours, so maybe.'

The lift doors opened.

Seb stepped out. 'If there's food involved, it sounds good to me!'

CHAPTER 13
FOLLOW YOUR GUT

The friends stood on the pavement by the athletes' promenade. Hannah stared down the pencil-straight road, where flags ran down either side. She'd read about this promenade in her guidebook: each flag that sailed in the wind represented a nation competing at the Games. As cool as the athletes' promenade was, there was no time to take photos. Hannah followed signs to navigate their way to the nearest bus stop. She watched as a minibus came round the corner. Seb waved his hand about, while Maria leaned into the road.

The bus came to a halt. They stepped on board, and Hannah suddenly realized there was no driver – just seats facing opposite each other. She turned to her friends, raising her eyebrows.

'Driverless!' Maria said. 'I've heard about these!'

'So cool,' Hannah breathed.

It was empty apart from two Spaniards and someone Hannah thought might be a Costa Rican. Hannah recognized the red-and-yellow-striped flag of Spain but wasn't totally sure of the blue-red-and-white one.

'Okay.' Hannah lowered her voice as they took a bench by the window. 'I think we're safe to talk about the investigation.'

Seb looked around. 'At least there aren't any Americans to figure us out.'

'Let's plan what we're going to ask Jesse.' Hannah took out her notebook. 'We could ask him what it's like having all the media behind the scenes. Hopefully he'll tell us some stories about what happened after the ceremony.'

'He might even talk about Machi,' said Maria.

'And if we find out that he didn't see Machi yesterday,' Hannah said, 'we might be able to rule her out.'

'But what if she had an accomplice?' she asked.

'Then we can ask whether he's going to be part of any documentaries.'

'We could try and get him to talk about Marcus too,' said Maria.

The bus slowed down at a zebra crossing and let some American athletes across the road.

'We could ask him about the relay,' said Hannah. 'You know, "How's the team feeling about the final tonight?"'

Seb chuckled. 'It's not an interview. You're not reporting for the BBC!'

'Okay, so what would you say?'

'I don't know... Something like, "Do you reckon you've got a chance in the final tonight?"'

'That's way too open!'

'That's just the icebreaker,' he said. 'After that we can ask whether he saw the guys last night.'

'Ooh, I see!' Hannah nodded. 'Then we'll know whether he saw Marcus.'

The bus stopped outside the food hall and Maria got

to her feet. 'We could even find out when the medal went missing.'

They each hopped off the bus and stood outside the entrance to the food hall.

'Wow!' Hannah looked up at her reflection in the long mirrored windows. 'How is it so big?'

'It's even better than I thought it'd be!' Maria squealed. 'The actual Tokyo food hall!'

Hannah watched the athletes, coaches and all kinds of other team members walk in and out of the double doors. The trio entered what seemed to Hannah like the world's largest cloakroom. There were several volunteers working on stalls, collecting people's bags and stashing them in giant storage racks. At least it was cool in here from the air-con, thought Hannah, though she still wished she didn't have to wear this jacket. She led her friends past the desks and up to a group of smiling faces in blue uniforms.

'Would you like to eat upstairs or downstairs?' one of them asked.

Where would Jesse have gone?

Maria itched towards the escalator. 'My gut instinct says upstairs.'

Hannah watched a cluster of South Koreans in white kit joking around on an escalator as they made their way to the upper floor. 'I guess if you're going to follow your gut, you should do it in a food hall!'

They joined the escalator and Hannah crossed her fingers. Hopefully, luck would be on their side. They really needed to find Jesse soon.

When they reached the top, Hannah didn't know where to look first. The buffet counter stretched all the way round the room with rows and rows of tables in the middle. 'Where do we even start?!'

Maria followed the swarm of people stepping off the escalator. 'How about we get some food and then try to find Jesse's table . . .'

Hannah scanned the room for Americans, spotting pockets of them everywhere. 'What if we get caught eating food that's not for us?'

Seb laughed. 'I don't think the food would be the problem. More the breaking and entering?'

'He's right,' said Maria. 'And it'd look weird if we came here and didn't eat . . .'

'You're right,' Hannah said to Maria. 'We'll get something small.' She wasn't that hungry after all the sushi earlier. Seb picked up a tray and she followed behind him. 'What next?'

Seb looked around. 'That girl in green just took

some cutlery from there.' He ran over to a nearby rack and fetched knives and forks. He dropped them on Hannah's and Maria's trays with a grin. 'I guessed that you wouldn't be using chopsticks.'

Hannah smirked. 'I won't be using a knife either.' She waggled her empty jacket sleeve.

'Oh, I didn't think. I'm so sorry!'

She smiled. 'Don't be silly! There's nothing to be sorry about.' She turned to the vast hall of counters and cuisines. 'Any idea where we go from here?'

'This is kinda like the food hall at the Youth Games. Just a much bigger version.' Maria pointed to the signs above each section of the buffet. 'It depends what you fancy. It looks like they have pretty much everything here!'

Hannah took in the signs. There was an Asian section in purple, Mediterranean in blue, Japanese in pink, and allergies in red.

Hannah suddenly felt hungry again. 'There's so much choice! How could anyone ever eat it all?'

'Is that a challenge?' Seb grinned. 'Best one yet!' He slid his tray along the buffet bar and introduced himself to the food staff. 'Hey there.' He beamed. 'I'll take one of everything.'

The server managed to balance an assortment of

149

vegetables on a plate and hand it over to Seb. Before he left, he turned to Hannah and Maria and hissed, 'I know what I can do.' He leaned in a little closer. 'I can ask the staff if they know who was at yesterday's dinner.'

'Good idea!' said Maria. 'But be subtle.'

'I can be subtle.' Seb winked. 'Watch this.' He waved to the next servers, dressed in purple. 'Hi!'

They eagerly waved back. 'Hello!'

'Gee!' Hannah watched as Seb surveyed all the options, from chow mein to chicken tikka. 'I could spend all day here!'

One of the servers sighed. 'We do – the food hall is open all day, every day.'

'You must work so hard! But at least you saw the dinner with Jesse Marks, right?'

'He should be a spy with improv that good,' Hannah whispered to Maria.

The server shook her head. 'Ah, no, I missed it. Yesterday was my day off.'

'Oh, that's a shame.'

Hannah gave Maria a nudge. 'A real shame.'

Seb didn't let that stop him from ordering a portion of Thai noodles. Hannah's stomach was rumbling now.

'And some onion bhajis, please!' she added.

Maria held up her fingers. 'For two!'

The lady filled another plate and passed it to Seb. He pushed the tray along and eyed up the next section. 'Mediterranean, anyone?'

Hannah was almost drooling over the pizza, pasta and paella. 'Seeing as we're only here once . . . Well, Seb and I are only here once – but you'll be competing at the next Games, Maria, and eating this every day!'

Maria blushed.

Seb moved his gaze to the servers. 'And it gives me a chance to find a volunteer who knows about that dinner. There must be one somewhere!'

CHAPTER 14
EAT FAST

Maria and Hannah went to find a seat while Seb circled the room collecting food.

Hannah had just finished writing up her latest notes when a tray hit the table.

'Man!' Seb groaned.

Maria watched him sit down. 'No luck?'

'None! They either weren't there last night or didn't speak English. But that's not the worst news.'

Hannah felt her heart dip, waiting for the disappointment. Had someone found the medal first? 'What is it?'

'When I was talking to one of the servers, she said that she saw Jesse in here an hour ago.'

Maria shook her head. 'That means there's no way he's still here.' She looked at Seb's tray pointedly. 'Unless he picked up as much stuff as you!'

Then Hannah's stomach growled so loudly that Seb pushed the tray of food into the middle of the table. 'Take your pick.'

She forced a smile and helped herself to the ravioli. 'Thanks.'

Just as Hannah was putting a forkful of pasta to her mouth, she heard an American accent call out behind them.

'Hey!'

She spun round to see an athlete coming towards them on a skateboard. 'No! Who's that guy?'

Maria stuffed her accreditation inside her jacket. 'I don't know!'

The older boy with long, shaggy hair jumped off the board and tucked it under his arm. He placed a hand on Maria's back. 'Hey, Ja—' He took a step back. 'Oh . . . you're not Jasmine.'

'Hmm, yeah, we get mistaken for each other a lot.' Maria gave a nervous laugh.

'Mind if I join you?' He smiled. 'I'm Fred, by the way.'

'Um . . . sure,' Seb said in his New Yorker accent. 'I'm Seb, and this is Hannah and Maria.'

Hannah wondered why he'd given their real names, but then realized they couldn't use the ones from the accreditation – in case this Fred guy knew Anastasia, Cam or Nina. She tucked her lanyard away, like Maria had done. 'Hey there!' she said in her best American accent.

She cringed at the sound of her own voice. *Hey there??*

Okay, so she was going to have to bite her tongue. One slip of her accent and it was game over.

'Back in a minute!' Fred disappeared off towards a fridge full of drinks.

'Shall we make excuses and go?' said Maria. 'He might realize we're not real athletes!'

Hannah pointed to the food in front of them and side-eyed Seb. 'We can't just leave all this food – it'll look suspicious to just abandon it. Plus we can't waste it.'

'Don't worry!' said Seb through a mouthful of noodles. 'I can eat fast!'

Fred returned with an armful of drinks.

'You may as well take one of these each. They're free!'

Seb lunged across the table and passed a bottle each to the girls.

As Hannah squashed the bottle into her satchel, she whispered to Maria, 'Do you know much about skateboarding?'

She nodded. 'Kinda.'

'In that case, it's your turn to do the talking.'

Maria sat up and turned to Fred.

'So, how did you do in the park final yesterday?'

'Pretty good.' A grin crept across his mouth. 'I won silver.'

'That's amazing!' Maria high-fived him. 'Do you have any more events?'

'Nah.' Fred took a sip from his drink. 'Us skateboarders have already started celebrating.'

'What did you do?' Seb said in his American accent.

'I got to go to a special US team dinner!'

'But wasn't that for athletes who've been to three Games?' Maria asked. 'And skateboarding is new to the Games.'

Fred nodded. 'You're right, but I have been to three. I used to be a snowboarder and I've been to two winter Games.'

'Oh, cool!' Seb winked at Hannah and Maria. Hannah knew what it meant: *See, getting all this food and not being able to leave yet was a good thing!*

Hannah blurted, 'Who else was there?'

Now Seb elbowed her. 'Accent!' he whispered.

But it didn't seem to matter – Fred didn't bat an eyelid.

'So many people!' he said, grinning. 'Jesse, Marcus, even the Japanese prime minister!'

As Fred showed Maria his selfie with Jesse, Hannah murmured to Seb, 'Ask if it was being filmed?'

'Hey, Fred,' Seb said, 'it sounds epic. Are we ever gonna get to see the dinner?'

'I think so. A lady was doing a lot of filming.' He lowered his voice and the others leaned in. 'Between you and me, she was a monster!'

As he showed them the rest of his photos, Hannah was itching to ask questions. She fetched her phone from her pocket and sent Seb a message from under the table: *Find out if it was Machi.*

Seb's phone beeped and he looked down to read the message. He sent a quick thumbs-up emoji back to

Hannah and stashed the phone back in his pocket.

'What were you saying?' Seb asked. 'About the lady filming stuff?'

'Oh yeah! I couldn't tell what she was saying. It was all in Japanese, but I knew it was mean.' He puffed out his cheeks. 'Her poor assistant.'

'Who else was there?' asked Maria.

'There were some really important Japanese people.' Fred rubbed his chin. 'I think the Games president was there... and the sports secretary... and the one for media... A Japanese princess, the US ambassador to Japan, a Tokyo movie star.'

'Jeez, a proper VIP guest list!' Maria laughed.

'I know, right? The security was insane!'

'Seems like they were guarding the wrong people!' Seb dared to joke as he swallowed a bite of pizza.

Fred cocked his head to the side. 'What?'

Seb shuffled in his seat. 'You know.' He gave a nervous laugh. 'Jesse and his medal.'

'Oh yeahhh.' Fred fiddled with his pocket. 'Someone could have just taken the medal from his jacket in all the bustle.'

'Did he have it in his pocket?' asked Maria.

'I don't know for sure. I'm just guessing he did. You

know, you ask a lot of questions.' Fred's eyes narrowed. 'You're not trying to find it, are you?'

'Uh . . .' Maria gave a sheepish smile.

'I knew it!' Fred rocked his chair back. 'Good for you! Someone has to earn the cash reward.' He swung forward and sighed. 'Man, I wish I could stay and help you, but my flight is tonight, which sucks.' His phone began to ring. 'Uh, that's my coach. I gotta go.' He stood up and rolled his skateboard from under the table. 'Nice to meet you!'

They waved as Fred skated away, his phone to his ear.

'Phew!' Hannah fell back into her chair. 'That could have been a disaster.'

'It's a good job he didn't ask any questions about us!' Seb said, munching on a slice of cake.

Hannah took her notebook out again. 'We got some good information, although I don't like how many people were at that dinner.' She clicked her pen. 'The thief could be anyone! Can you remember who he named? All I can remember is—'

Maria's hand shot up. 'I can!'

Hannah turned a new page and held her pen at the ready. 'Perfect! Hit me with them!'

'The prime minister.'

'Unlikely, but we'll write him down.'

'Film stars.'

'Also unlikely, but still, let's try and find out which ones.'

'The US ambassador to Japan.'

Seb chuckled to himself. 'You never know with politicians.'

'Didn't he say Machi was there?' Hannah remembered aloud.

'And Marcus,' Seb added.

Maria pushed up her glasses. 'I'd understand if Marcus didn't post anything about the dinner, but why didn't Machi post anything? She's ALWAYS posting.'

'And surely she'd want to post about an exclusive event?' Hannah said.

Seb shrugged. 'Maybe if it's part of her documentary, it's under embargo?'

'Under what?' Maria asked.

'Embargo. It's a professional word for *top secret*.'

Hannah's phone began to ring and she pulled it from her pocket. She looked down at the caller ID and gasped.

'Oh, no no no!

'Who is it?' asked Seb.

Hannah showed the others her phone. 'It's my dad!'

CHAPTER 15
TOP KNOT

Hannah answered the call.

'Hi, Dad!'

'How's the tour? You've been gone ages!'

She looked around for a clock and spotted the watch on Maria's wrist, quickly checking the time.

'Yeah, it's great,' she replied. 'We've gone all around the Sportpark!'

'I didn't realize you were going that far! The qualifiers finish at two.'

Thank god he didn't know how far they'd really gone.

'But we're on our way back now,' said Hannah.

'Whereabouts are you?'

'Uh . . .' She turned to the others. 'We're in a special athlete bit.' At least that wasn't a lie.

'Lucky you! In which venue?'

Hannah tried to picture the map of the Sportpark. 'The hockey stadium!' she said. Okay, so that definitely *was* a fib.

'Oh.' Her dad sighed. 'That's the other end of the Sportpark! You're going to miss all of the qualifiers.'

'We're going as fast as we can!'

'Don't worry. Just stick with the tour guide and come back in one piece.'

'Thanks, Dad.'

'I'll see you in a bit.'

'See ya!'

She stashed her phone into her pocket.

'We need to get back to the stadium.'

'Shoot, is your dad angry?' asked Maria.

'No, but I can tell he'll be sad if we miss the whole morning session.'

Seb looked around. 'How long do we have left?'

'An hour,' said Hannah.

'Right . . . He nodded. So let's get going.'

They made their way back down the escalator and out on to the pavement. The floods of people coming in and out of the food hall for lunch made it livelier than ever.

Maria hurried over the zebra crossing. 'Over here!' She gestured over to her right. 'That sign says the athlete buses are that way.'

Hannah's eyes followed the road along the edge of the village. It was perfectly straight and much wider than any of the others.

'This must be the main road in and out of here.' She watched uniformed people with glow sticks ushering vehicles to the far end of the road. 'They must be traffic wardens!'

'I bet they control people coming in and out,' said Maria.

Seb nodded. 'Do you want to walk over or catch a driverless bus?'

Hannah took another look at Maria's watch. 'We'd better walk. We don't know exactly where those buses go and we don't have time to go the wrong way.'

The trio set off quickly down the main road, walking by hundreds of flag-draped balconies on their right. They smiled as they passed athletes from every nation. Well . . . every nation but one. Whenever they spotted an American kit, they kept their heads down and their gazes low. Eventually Hannah spotted another signpost.

'Bus stop straight ahead,' she said. 'Looks like we guessed right.'

They passed the South African block, where a group of coaches were playing a game of cricket outside. Hannah watched as the woman batting smacked what was definitely a six in their direction.

'Heads up!' she yelled.

Hannah dodged out of the way as Maria lunged for the ball.

'Mine!' Maria shouted, and the ball fell neatly into her hands.

She tossed it back to the coaches and the woman smiled. 'Not bad! You should play for your country!'

Maria laughed and turned to the others. 'I have no idea what they're playing.'

They kept walking and Seb explained cricket.

'So it's kinda like baseball, but you just keep running back and forth?' Maria asked.

Seb laughed. 'Yeah, but no . . . When we're done finding the medal, I'll teach you how to play.'

Hannah saw the end of the road ahead. It was blocked off by a huge metal barrier, with a blue tent on each end. Behind the barrier was an endless queue of buses.

'That's it!' she said. 'That's the bus stop!'

'We made it!' Maria grinned.

Hannah watched a fresh batch of athletes from a bus enter through a tent on the right. Just like the spectators in the stadium, they too had to walk through airport-style checks.

'It's funny, isn't it?' Hannah said.

'What is?' asked Maria.

She lowered her voice. 'The fact that they have all those security checks and we managed to sneak in.'

Seb pointed to the guard leading the checks – an athletic man with a top knot on the crest of his head. 'Look at that guy! He's tall, ripped and got all the fancy gear, but we outsmarted him.'

'He's wasting his time as a guard,' Maria joked. 'He should be a basketball player instead!'

They eventually arrived at the checkpoint. But on the other side of the tent, Hannah realized that there wasn't just one bus queue, but three! She looked down the first queue at all the volunteers standing along the path.

'What's all this?' Seb gawped.

Hannah tried to piece it all together. Outside each bus was a volunteer holding a picture of a sport. 'It looks like each bus goes to a different venue. We just have to find the card for athletics.'

She scanned the line of cards held aloft – hockey, swimming, cycling . . . and was that sailing? Finally her eye caught on a picture of a runner beside a javelin thrower.

'That must be it!' Just as Hannah said it, the man grasping the card took a look at his watch and gave a nod to the driver. 'It's about to leave!'

'Wait!' Seb waved at the driver. 'Wait for us!'

The volunteer made eye contact with Hannah as she charged towards him. He turned to the driver, who was now closing the doors. 'Woah, woah, wait!' He stuck out a hand and forced the doors back open.

Maria grabbed hold of the railing and swung up the step. 'Thank you!' she panted.

Hannah unfastened her pin badge and handed it to the volunteer just as she stepped on.

'*Arigato gozaimasu*,' she said, smiling. *Thank you* was one of the Japanese phrases that Hannah had learned on the plane.

He bowed his head.

Seb clambered on last. They quickly filled the seats behind Maria and the bus set off for the stadium.

Seb pointed to Hannah's lanyard. 'I can't believe you donated your pin badge!'

'He deserved it. Without him, we'd be so late!'

Maria popped her head over the seats. 'So, where are we?'

Seb chuckled. 'I take it you mean, "Where are we with the Gold Medal Mystery?"'

'Yeah.'

'Well...' Hannah tried to forget her dad's potential

wrath and pulled out her notebook. 'So far our suspects are everybody at the dinner.' She circled one of the names. 'Our prime suspect is now Marcus.'

'I thought we would have found the thief by now,' said Seb, pulling a face.

'We're not *too* far away from catching the thief,' Maria whispered. 'We probably know more than the police – I bet they don't know exactly how Marcus feels about Jesse.'

'It's just annoying that we didn't have time to find the guest dining room.' Hannah turned to a new page. 'I know it was a long shot, but we could've found something huge.'

'So where do we go next?' said Seb.

'We need to find the documentary-makers,' she said. 'I feel like getting hold of yesterday's footage is the only way forward.'

'Where do we find them?' Maria asked.

'If there are finals on, they'll definitely be in the underground athlete zone.'

'At least we can get in there now.' Seb waved his accreditation.

'Oh yeah!' Hannah grinned. 'We're athletes now.' She bit her nails, thinking about her dad waiting.

Would there even be any time to find the documentary-makers? She'd have to work out a way somehow! She pulled her hand away from her mouth. She had to stop biting her nails!

CHAPTER 16
THAT IS LIFE

The bus was soon arriving on the athletes' side of the stadium. It passed the scanners at the entrance to the Sportpark and followed the long loop round. When it reached the stadium, the driver turned right down a slope and into a tunnel.

'There's no way we could have found this ourselves!' Seb whispered to the girls.

The bus stopped beside the pavement and Hannah smiled. 'It's literally a secret tunnel.'

Everybody began to file off the bus and the three friends followed closely behind, wanting to make sure they got into the stadium safely.

They followed a German athlete through some sliding doors and suddenly heard applause from the volunteers.

They're cheering the athletes as they arrive! Hannah

realized. She gave them a wave as she walked past, grinning. 'I feel so important!' she said to her friends.

Maria leaned over and squealed. 'Damn, this makes me want to compete in a Games even more!'

'Your second Games . . .' Hannah winked.

'Yes!' Maria nodded. 'Because I'm obviously competing here.'

They walked through another set of sliding doors and into a foyer. It was pretty empty with just a desk in the centre and some volunteers surrounding a whiteboard. In the far corner a media team was setting up a camera while a presenter rehearsed his lines. Hannah looked around to see where the other athletes were going. Most of them were heading left through another set of doors.

'Hey, Maria,' she said.

'Yeah?'

'What's the time?'

'One thirty-three.'

Hannah felt her chest tighten. 'The shot put only has twenty-seven minutes left. We're going to miss all of it!'

Seb looked around. 'Okay, so . . . where are the stands . . . That way? Wait, no.'

Hannah turned to a bending corridor on her right and

noticed a sign hanging from the ceiling. She ran her eyes down the list:

Call Room 1
Call Room 2
Technical Office
Athlete Stadium Seating

'This way!' They ran down the nearly empty corridor. As they passed each door, however, Hannah realized that the stadium was anything but calm.

Through the first door, she saw officials in white shirts huddled around a computer, and volunteers were dashing to and fro with sheets of paper. Athletes were lining up outside one room and there was a lot of shouting coming from another. Hannah caught a glimpse of something white and crumpled on the floor. It looked like a note folded into the shape of a crane. She picked it up to read it, but it was all in Japanese. She couldn't see a bin nearby, so she stuffed it into her pocket.

She peered through the next door. Inside the room were volunteers all dressed in the same outfit – white slacks with baby-blue jackets. In front of them a woman with a headset was handing them each a cushion. Before Hannah could look any closer, a door on the other side swung open and a herd of people with cameras and microphones came flooding into the corridor.

Maria stepped back against the wall. 'Who are all these people?'

'Press?' Hannah tried to catch a glimpse of the athlete amongst it all. She spied someone at the centre of the throng with dark hair and a navy-blue collar.

'Do you think it's Jesse?' said Maria, following Hannah's gaze.

'I don't know. They look like they're heading for that conference room over there.'

As the press fought their way inside, the corridor began to quieten down. The three of them joined the back of the huddle and Seb poked his head through the conference-room door.

'No, no, sorry.' A volunteer blocked him off with her arm and frowned. 'No entry. Press only.'

'But—' Seb argued. 'I need to see my dad! He's a presenter.'

Quick thinking, thought Hannah.

The volunteer shook her head. 'You have to wait to get access to the media side.'

Seb turned to the others. 'This whole place must be split into sections!' He swung back to the volunteer. 'How many sections are there?'

'Spectators on ground floor and level one. Athlete seating, just ground floor,' she replied. 'Athlete preparation, one half of lower ground; media on the other.'

Hannah shot the volunteer a smile. 'Do you know how we can get to the other side?'

'Through the conference room.' The volunteer tapped her accreditation. 'But only for media passes.'

'Right . . .' Hannah took a step back and mumbled, 'That was a waste of time.'

'This place is such a maze!' said Seb.

'I think we should get back to my dad,' Hannah said, checking her phone for the time: one forty-five. 'We can't take any more detours!'

'Look!' Maria nodded towards an athlete dressed in blue and yellow, walking in their direction.

Hannah thought the woman looked familiar, with her slick blonde hair and cat-like eyes. If only she could remember who the pretty face and broad shoulders belonged to.

The girl stopped outside the conference room and sighed.

'Oh, am I too late?'

'Depends,' said the volunteer. 'Oksana?'

She nodded.

'They are ready for you.' The volunteer opened the door.

The shot put had finished early! That was the last thing Hannah needed.

The shot putter started to make her way inside and Hannah lunged after her. 'Ooh, Oksana!'

She stepped back into the corridor. 'Yes?'

'Can I take a photo of you, please?'

'Of course!' She smiled.

Hannah pulled out her camera from her satchel. 'My dad is going to love this!' It would be the perfect excuse for why it took so long to get back.

The volunteer held up her hand. 'Ms Mereshko, they need you now.'

'They can wait,' she said. 'Young athletes are more important.'

The volunteer fell quiet and Oksana posed for Hannah's camera.

'You want me to strike a pose?'

'Do whatever you like!'

Hannah snapped away and Oksana raised her hands into a shrug. 'Like this?'

'That's perfect!'

Hannah couldn't wait to show her dad the photos. They could make up for missing the morning session.

She lowered her camera and grinned.

'Thank you so much! You're amazing!'

'Thank you!' Oksana lingered in the doorway. 'American, right?'

'Half American, half British,' Hannah quickly lied. She'd completely forgotten about trying to put on an American accent.

'You have an American pin badge?' she asked.

Hannah flashed her lanyard. 'Not right now, but I have an official Tokyo Games badge.'

'Cool! Want to swap?'

'I have one too!' said Seb, reaching for his pocket. Hannah gave him a prod and he tailed off. 'But so does Maria – she can swap this time.'

'Aw thanks.' Maria stepped forward and handed over her pin to Oksana.

'Now I don't have to buy one!' the Ukrainian joked. 'And . . .' She unfastened a pin from her accreditation. 'I give you a special badge. Take care of it.'

Maria blushed, taking the badge. 'Thank—'

'Ms Mereshko,' the volunteer pleaded, her voice higher now.

'Ooh!' Oksana waved goodbye. 'They really, really need me.'

She followed the volunteer and the door closed behind them.

'Oh wow!' Seb squawked. 'That was epic!'

Hannah tried to sneak a peek at the pin. 'What did she give you?'

Maria opened up her palm. 'I don't know,' she said, squinting. 'It looks a little rusty. Or is it meant to be that colour?'

'I bet it's an old one! From LA or Mexico!' Hannah loved anything to do with history.

'I know,' said a Japanese voice.

The three friends turned around.

'I recognized it as soon as I saw it.' A boy who looked around their age sat perched on a ledge beside the water fountain. His thick, dark hair covered his eyes as he spoke.

Maria tossed the badge into the air like a coin. 'You really know?'

The boy brushed the hair from his eyes. 'I might need to look again.'

She brought the pin badge over to the fountain and let him take a closer look.

'Yes!' His words echoed down the almost empty corridor. 'I was right. It is a badge from Japan.'

'From the sixties?' asked Hannah. 'I read about that Games on the plane...' Hannah trailed off. She realized she'd forgotten to use an American accent again, although the boy hadn't seemed to notice.

The boy shook his head. 'Before then. Years ago, we should have had the Games, but there was a war and it never happened.'

'But all the merchandise was still made?' Seb asked, doing his New Yorker accent.

The boy nodded. 'They made it so early, it was too late to stop.'

Maria smiled. 'How do you know all this?'

The boy sat swinging his legs. 'I am the son of a director. I have seen lots of documentaries about Japan.'

Seb took a seat next to him. 'You're Machi Mari's son?'

'No!' he said. 'You think that she is my mom?'

'I can't see her being anyone's mum.'

The boy laughed. 'Ha ha, true.'

'So, whose son are you?' asked Maria.

'I am Onishi Shig's son.' He lowered his voice. 'The organizers gave us special access to the Games for my dad's new documentary, but he told me not to say anything.'

'Why's that?' she asked.

'He says, "Ren, you are not allowed to brag! It is rude."'

Maria chuckled. 'Well, don't worry. We won't tell anyone you told us.'

'Thank you.'

Seb shuffled closer. 'What sort of stuff has your dad directed?'

'Movies, royal family stuff, programmes about famous people.' He grinned. 'Basically, anything about Japan.'

'Epic! Do you get to go to the film sets too?'

'I did.' He sighed. 'But not now. My dad says now the new directors are stealing the old directors' jobs.'

'That sucks.' Maria frowned.

'That is life.' He shrugged. 'And sport. New athletes eventually overtake the old ones.'

Hannah was glad that Seb and Maria were doing all the talking. The boy's English was so good, he would easily recognize her accent. Clearly Seb had thought the same thing.

'Hey, how is your English so good?' Seb asked Ren.

The boy smiled. 'First, thank you. And second, I go to an international school.'

The door to the conference room reopened and Hannah tried to peek inside. She spotted a short, slender man in a linen shirt and slacks. He nodded to the volunteer on the door.

'Hey, Dad!' The boy bowed.

Hannah watched the man closely. So this was Onishi Shig.

He walked over to the group and bowed.

'Ah, hello! I hope Ren has not taken too much of your time.'

'Not at all!' Seb shook his head. 'We like chatting with him.'

Hannah glanced at her phone: 14.11. Not only was the shot put finished, but all the other sports would now be too. They really needed to get back to her dad . . .

'Well, thank you for making Ren welcome,' Onishi said. 'I know you athletes have strict schedules.'

'Of course!' Seb put on his diplomat smile, although he was still speaking with an American twang. 'It's a pleasure! He actually knows more about the Games than we do!'

'He is a bit of a fanatic,

and it is nice for him to meet some younger athletes.'
Onishi looked them up and down. 'You do look young.'

'We're thirteen,' Seb lied. 'You know how young they
start us gymnasts! Ren's told us loads about you,' Seb
went on. Hannah guessed he was quickly changing the
subject. 'Your work sounds amazing.'

Onishi brought his hand to his chest. 'Ah, you are
too kind. It is the crew that makes it so fantastic.' He
brought his hands together. 'Ah, I could talk to you
all day, but unfortunately we need to go.' He nodded
to the conference room. 'Come on, Ren, we'll go
through here.'

Ren jumped down and bowed to his new friends.
'Bye . . . Oh, wait . . . I don't know your names.'

'Cam, Nina and Anastasia.' Seb grinned.

Ren turned to his dad. 'Can we invite them to
the parade?'

'Parade?' Seb's eyes lit up.

'Oh yes! There is a parade tomorrow,' Onishi told the
trio, 'to celebrate Japanese culture during the Games.
We're looking for as many athletes as possible to be on
the sports float.'

'That would be epic!'

'Great!' Onishi brought his hands together again.

Hannah nudged Seb as subtly as she could manage. They couldn't go to a parade with other athletes and risk getting found out. Plus, how was that going to help them solve the medal mystery? 'Uh . . . actually . . . we can't do it tomorrow. We're . . . uh . . . competing.'

Onishi tilted his head to the side. 'Oh, what a shame.'

'Yeah,' Maria sighed. 'Today is our only day off.'

'Well, good luck tomorrow,' Ren said. 'It was nice to meet you.'

As he and his dad strode off into the conference room, Seb called out behind them.

'Wait!'

Ren turned around with a grin. 'Yeah?'

'I can give you my number? We could stay in touch and maybe meet up after the Games.'

Ren pulled out his phone from his pocket. 'Epic!'

Hannah wondered if he'd picked the word up from Seb. It was a good idea of Seb's to share his number – maybe they could get footage from Onishi if they stayed in touch. But wait . . .

'You don't have an American phone number!' she whispered in Seb's ear.

He shook his head.

'The team has been given Games phones, so you can

have my Japanese number.' Seb read a number aloud and Ren noted it in his phone.

'Thank you, Cam. I'll see you later.'

'Bye!'

The door closed behind them.

'Was that a fake number?' Hannah asked, confused.

'No, don't worry – this is a Japanese phone from my dad's work.'

'That makes sense. And good thinking – we might be able to get footage from Onishi if we make friends with Ren.'

'Ha, I didn't even think of that!' Seb said.

Maria looked at her watch. 'Ah, Hannah . . .'

Her dad. He'd been waiting ages! Even her photo with Oksana couldn't explain why they'd been gone for so long. She felt sick with dread.

'We need to find my dad! Right now!'

CHAPTER 17
ATTENTION

Hannah rushed back towards the foyer. 'We need to find a way upstairs!'

'Upstairs?' said Seb, breaking into a run.

'Yeah, into the stands!'

The trio passed door after door, until the *ding* of a lift echoed out.

Hannah followed the noise to a small lift beside the athletes' entrance. 'Over there!' she yelled, and they all dived in.

The lift couldn't move fast enough for Hannah. Even the doors seemed to take ages to close and then it dawdled up to the second floor. Eventually, the doors opened and they were greeted by thousands of voices singing along to the music blaring out. The sound made the hairs on Hannah's neck stand up, but there was no time to hang around and take in the atmosphere.

The three of them ran to the nearest block of seats and Hannah searched for its allocated letter.

Then she realized. 'We're on the wrong side! This bit is just for athletes.'

She ran down into the concourse, Seb and Maria following. Instead of sushi bars and gift shops, the athletes had personalized merch stands and pin-swap stations. A little further round, Hannah saw a games zone with air hockey and Xboxes. After they had passed several stalls of free goodies and gadgets, a small, guarded barrier came into sight.

'That must be the end of the athletes' section!'

Maria hung back. 'How do we get past the lady?'

Hannah bit a nail. 'We should change back into our normal clothes.'

'Sure . . . Why are we doing that?'

'You heard the volunteer talk about all the sections. There is no way an athlete will be able to walk past those guards.'

'So we're just normal people again?'

'Yes.'

Maria slumped. 'Oh, I liked being an athlete.'

Hannah unzipped her jacket. 'And I like not being in

trouble with my dad.' She gasped. 'I hadn't even thought about what he'd say if he saw us in this!' At least she no longer had to hide the fact she only had one arm. Although, she had a bad feeling that it wouldn't be the last time . . .

The trio ran to the nearest bathroom and swapped their team kit for their normal clothes that they'd stuffed into their bags. Hannah emerged on to the concourse first and waited for the others.

'Quick!' she shouted.

'I'm going as fast as I can!' hissed Seb, as Maria popped out of the bathroom too.

They made their way to the barrier.

As soon as the volunteer on guard laid eyes on the gang, she hurried over in a panic.

'You're not athletes? You're not supposed to be here!'

'I'm so sorry!' Seb said, back in diplomat mode. 'We were trying to find the gift shop and we got lost!'

The guard waved them along. 'You must come through here!'

'Thank you.' Hannah smiled, relief flooding through her. 'We've been trying to find our way back for ages.'

The guard opened up the gate and ushered the friends through to the other side.

'Well,' Maria said, skipping towards the nearest stadium map. 'That was kinda easy.'

Seb laughed. 'I don't think the guard was even listening to us.'

'Sorry, what did you say?' Maria said.

'You heard me the first time!'

'He's becoming immune to your tricks, Maria,' Hannah teased.

She shook her head. 'I've got plenty up my sleeve.'

'Anyway...' Hannah turned to the map. 'Where's Block H?'

Maria pointed to the closest set of stairs. 'Up there.'

As they climbed the steps, a line of Japanese school children came walking down in single file. One of them waved to Hannah and giggled. Hannah raised her arm to wave back and her satchel slipped from her shoulder. It tumbled down the stairs and its contents spilled out on to the floor.

'Stupid bag!' she called out, chasing after it, but her notes and kit were already scattered across the floor.

'Wow!' one of the children gasped. 'American clothes!' The rest of the class crowded around Hannah as she tried to stuff everything back into her bag.

'You Jesse know?' asked another girl.

She gave an awkward laugh. 'Ah, no, I don't.'

'His medal missing!'

The girl's friend chimed in too. 'My sister say he hide.'

'Really?' Hannah paused and looked up at them, intrigued.

'It true,' the girl said in her broken English. 'She say he for attention do it.'

'Attention?' Hannah buckled her bag shut. 'Of course!'

She waved to the children. 'Thank you.'

They all waved back. 'Byeee!'

Hannah ran up the stairs and joined Seb and Maria, who were at the top, looking around for her.

'What happened to you?' asked Seb. 'Everything okay?'

'Yes, fine. I just dropped my bag in front of a load of school kids.'

He shook his head. 'You should've told us! We could've helped.'

'I actually spoke to one of them . . . and she thought of something we missed.'

'What?' said Maria. 'We've been through everything, haven't we?'

Hannah moved away from the stairs to let people through. 'It seems some people are saying that the theft is one big publicity stunt.'

Maria scowled. 'Jesse would never do that!'

'It does seem unlikely,' Seb agreed.

'I know, but we have to explore every avenue and . . .'

Maria raised an eyebrow. 'And what?'

'He did do all that nice stuff for Haru . . . but you're right. He probably didn't do it.'

'He did those acts out of kindness.' Maria looked for back-up. 'Didn't he, Seb?'

Seb shoved his hands into his pockets.

'Seb?'

'Mmm.' He dragged his foot along the floor. 'I don't know.'

'Damn it, Seb! I thought you had me.' Maria turned to Hannah. 'I suppose you can add Jesse to the suspect list if you really have to.'

Hannah smiled. 'Thank you. I know it's hard to think with your head instead of your heart.'

Maria waved her hand. 'Well, it just means we've gotta work fast and prove he isn't guilty.'

'Sure . . .' Hannah jerked her head towards the entrance to Block H. 'Right after I tell my dad we're here and he takes us home.'

'What? Nooo!' Maria wailed.

Seb looked at Maria's watch. 'She's right. I've got to

get back to my dad. He'll be waiting for me.'

Hannah found her dad in the stands, just as the volunteers began to leave.

'Where on earth have you been?' he cried.

'We just met Oksana Mereshko!' said Hannah.

'What? How did you manage that?'

'It was part of Maria's tour,' she lied. It seemed like she was getting good at that.

Seb grinned. 'We saw her going to the conference room.'

Hannah's dad smiled. 'All right, I'll let you off for being late to meet me. I know I'm not cool to hang out with, but it's a shame you didn't see any of the shot put . . .'

Hannah pulled out her camera to distract her dad. 'Here you go!'

Her dad flicked through the photos. 'How fantastic is this!' He handed the camera back. 'Now let's get everybody back to their hotel before four o'clock.'

With Hannah's dad leading the way, the four of them left the stadium and emerged out into the bright sunshine. Hannah watched one of the blue-and-white fan buses drive away and turn towards the main road.

'Are we not getting a bus back?' she asked.

Her dad smiled. 'Mum's driver's here.' He pointed to a

small car park across the road. 'The car's just down there.'

Hannah marvelled at the array of fancy cars with their blacked-out windows and sleek, shiny bodywork. 'Cool! They sent one of these!'

They crossed the road and Maria's jaw dropped. 'You mean . . . you have people to drive you around . . . in cars like these?'

'Not all the time,' Hannah was quick to say. 'But sometimes when my mum works in another country, they give her a chauffeur.'

'Do we get to come back in one tomorrow?' Maria said. 'Please?'

'Well . . .' Hannah's dad said. 'If your parents haven't got anything planned for you.'

'Is that a yes?!' Hannah grinned. She'd been certain she'd be in more trouble for getting back late, but it looked as if their investigation would be able to carry on . . .

'I'm more than happy to take you all again,' he said. 'Maybe you'll watch some sport this time!'

'Thank you!' Maria squeaked.

Seb looked around the car park. 'So, which one is ours?'

'The cars usually have a flag of the country on them,' said Hannah.

He looked around at the sea of mini Japanese flags. 'I'm not sure that narrows it down.'

Her dad stopped beside a shiny black seven-seater Mercedes. '*Et voila!*' He opened the rear passenger door. 'Hop in.'

Seb dived in first, followed by Hannah and Maria.

'Cool! Leather seats!' Hannah said as they settled themselves in the back row.

'And TVs!' Maria gasped.

Someone turned around from the front passenger seat and beamed. 'You like it?' She brushed a strand of wispy blonde hair from her face.

'Mum!' Hannah beamed back. 'You're here!'

Her mum nodded. 'My meeting with the Japanese government finished early, so I thought I'd come to pick you up.' Her eyes darted between the friends sat on either side of Hannah. 'You two must be Seb and Maria.'

They both gave a friendly wave.

'Thanks for picking us up, Mrs Walker!' said Seb.

'Oh, it's no hassle.' She turned back around and spoke to the driver – a man wearing a black cap and a suit. 'I think we're ready to go, if that's okay.' She swung back again. 'Oh, and call me Nicola. If you need anything, just shout.'

The car began to trundle through the busy streets of Tokyo. Hannah's dad sat in the middle row of seats, leaning forward to listen to the radio commentary of the Games with her mum.

'Hey, Hannah,' said Maria. 'Can I see the photos of Oksana?'

'Yeah, sure!' She opened up her bag and pushed her team kit to the side. As she did so, she felt something crumple inside the pocket of the US jacket. 'Wait a minute . . .' She took out the slip of paper and set her satchel down.

'What's that?' whispered Seb.

Hannah checked to make sure her parents weren't watching. 'I found a note in the corridor of the athletes' section,' she explained.

'Where?' he asked.

'On the underground athlete level. It was outside a room with people in fancy outfits.'

'What else was in the room?' Maria asked.

'They had cushions.' Hannah chewed her lip. 'Like the ones they carry crowns on.'

Maria laughed. 'That's so British.'

Hannah suddenly sat upright. 'Of course – the cushions are for the medals! It's a note from the medal ceremony prep room.'

'Well, what does it say?' said Seb.

'I don't know – it's all in Japanese.'

'Oh,' Maria sighed.

Hannah unfurled the piece of paper. 'Do you think we can use a translation app to find out what it says—?'

'Yes!' Hannah's dad clapped his hands. 'He did it!' Hannah could hear the crowd cheering on the radio.

'He's definitely not listening to a word we're saying,' Hannah said.

Seb was already getting out his phone and opening a translation app. He scanned the piece of paper. Maria leaned over to read the results. She shook her head.

'Nothing?'

Hannah took a look at the screen. 'Is it not Japanese? I just assumed it was.' She turned to Seb. 'Try auto-detect.'

Seb switched the setting, but still no translation appeared. He nodded towards the driver. 'Could we ask him what it means?'

Hannah stole a glance to the front. Her mum was singing along to an advert. 'Mmm, I don't know. How do we ask without my parents finding out where we've been?'

'Say we found it on the concourse?' Seb suggested.

'I don't know, Seb.' Maria pushed up her glasses. 'Whatever is on that slip might prove we lied, and it's not like Hannah's dad knew where we really were.'

'You're right,' said Hannah 'It's too risky. I don't want to get into trouble and not be able to meet up tomorrow.'

The car pulled into a side street and Maria poked her head out of the window. 'Oh shoot.' She slipped back inside the car. 'My hotel's on this street!'

CHAPTER 18
TRANSLATOR

Fortunately, the gridlocked streets gave Maria some more time.

Hannah brought out her notebook. 'We need a plan for tomorrow.'

'How about we meet at the stadium?' Maria suggested. 'My family's going, so I can go with them and meet you there.'

'I think my dad has an interview he wants to take me to in the morning,' said Seb. 'I'm not sure I can get out of it. We'll be going to the stadium afterwards, though, so I can probably meet you at twelve thirty?'

'Sounds good,' Maria said. 'I can watch some stuff with my family before you get there.'

Hannah nodded. 'Me too. I don't want to let my dad down twice.' She turned to Seb. 'But, hang on . . .

how will you get in?'

'My dad's work gives me a stadium pass when I want to watch the athletics. I would have used one today, but they need time to prepare it.'

She nodded. 'Well, that's sorted.'

'Awesome!' Maria clapped her hands. 'We can keep going!'

'I just assumed we would!' Hannah laughed. 'I won't stop until we find the medal. We've got to catch the thief before anyone else does!'

'Or before one of us goes home . . .' added Maria.

'Nah, we'll find it by then!' Seb said.

Hannah continued writing in her notebook. 'Where should we go first tomorrow? Because I think—'

A loud ping from Seb's pocket cut Hannah off.

He pulled out his phone. 'It's a message from Ren!' He read it aloud. '*Hi, Cam. It's Ren! Nice to meet you today. I am sad we cannot see each other tomorrow, but good luck in your event!*'

Hannah smiled. 'Ah, that's sweet.'

'*It would be great to see you soon* —' Seb read out his reply as he typed – '*so let me know when you're free.*'

'Is this your plan to make friends with a director and get a job in a movie?' Maria teased.

'No! Well . . . maybe a little . . . but mainly to get the footage of Jesse!'

'Good idea,' said Hannah. 'But how are we going to do that?'

'How about this?' Seb started typing again, reading aloud as he went. *We'd love to see where you and your dad work!*

Hannah and Maria leaned closer and looked over Seb's shoulder. Ren began to type back an answer.

. . . Yes! That would be nice, Cam! The day after tomorrow? Seb quickly replied. *That's perfect! See you then!*

We can meet by the press room at 1.30 p.m., came Ren's reply.

Great! Seb typed.

Maria pointed to the phone. 'That's it!'

'That's what?' asked Hannah.

'Our translator! Ren can translate the note.'

'Yes! Wait, I'll send him a photo,' said Seb. Hannah passed him the slip of paper and he sent a message to Ren. 'Now we wait.'

'Hopefully he'll reply be—' Maria started to say.

Seb's phone began to ring. 'Wow, that was quick!' He answered it. 'Hi, Ren!'

Hannah held in a breath, waiting for what Ren would say.

CHAPTER 19
HIGH-TECH TOILET

Hannah put her ear to the other side of Seb's phone and listened in.

'Hi, Seb! I am happy to help.'

'Thanks so much!'

'The note says, *Men's one-hundred-metre ... bronze ... 8 p.m.*'

'That's it?'

'Yes, that is all. Where did you get it?'

'Han— I mean, Anastasia found it in the stadium.'

'Why did she pick it up?'

'Uh, we wondered whether it was a message from an athlete – you know, for a fan.'

'Oh ... I thought you were looking for secret messages.'

Seb gave a convincing laugh. 'Messages?'

'Yeah!' said Ren. 'Like a spy.'

'Ha, that would be funny!'

Hannah tapped Seb on the shoulder. '*Tell him,*' she mouthed.

Seb covered the phone with his hand. 'You sure?'

She nodded. 'He'll think we're finding it to help out a teammate. If anything, he'll want to join in and be more likely to help us with the footage!'

Seb returned the nod. 'Actually, Ren, we are. We were wondering whether you can help us.'

There was a squeal on the other end of the phone. 'I'd love to!'

Hannah saw Maria's eyes turn down and realized why. Now they'd have to split the reward four ways.

Hannah felt a pang of guilt. 'Oh, I didn't think about the reward . . . I'm sorry.'

'It's okay.' Maria gave her a small smile. 'Maybe we'll find the medal earlier with his help – if someone else beats us to it, we won't get any reward at all!'

Hannah thought about what Maria had told her at the Skytree. How expensive athletics was, how her dad needed a job. She looked up at her own parents – an interpreter and a foreign diplomat – sitting in this posh car, being driven around by a chauffeur.

'You know what,' she said, 'take my share.'

'Huh?'

'You said that athletics was expensive and your family shouldn't have to give everything up to do it.'

'No, you can't do that . . .'

'Maria, I insist. I'm not taking no for an answer!'

Maria wrapped her arms around her. 'You really mean it?'

'Yeah.' Hannah smiled. 'I really do.'

'Thank you. So much.'

That moment, the car pulled up in the driveway of a hotel.

'This is your hotel, isn't it, Maria?' Hannah's mum asked from the front.

She nodded. 'Yes, thank you.'

Hannah's dad jumped out of the car. 'I'll take you inside and make sure you find your parents.'

Seb quickly ended the call with Ren and turned to Hannah. 'Let's go too?'

Hannah nodded. 'Yeah, cool!'

'Well, in that case –' Hannah's mum unfastened her seatbelt – 'I don't want to be left out!'

The five of them entered the foyer. Hannah was blown away by the decor inside. Roman-style pillars ran from the marble floor to the glittering ceiling, and in the centre of the room hung strings of delicate fairy lights. She looked at her reflection in the floor and tapped her feet. She nudged Seb and performed a little made-up dance. 'I feel like I'm in a Fred Astaire movie!'

Maria rolled her eyes. 'I'll pretend I know who that is.'

Seb chuckled. 'Just picture every black-and-white movie you know.'

'Ah, okay.' She nodded. 'Just with a high-tech toilet.'

'Exactly!'

'Maria!' Maria's mum was walking towards them. She smiled at Hannah's parents. 'Thanks for bringing her back.'

'No problem!' Hannah's mum returned the smile.

'There's a bath waiting for you, Maria, if you want one,' her mum said.

'Yes, awesome! There's a TV in the bath,' she explained to Hannah and Seb. 'It's gotta be the best thing ever!'

Hannah laughed. 'Do you get American channels?'

'You get everything. Sports too!'

'I hate to break this up,' said Hannah's dad, 'but Seb needs to be back by four o'clock, otherwise I'll be in trouble!'

Maria tutted. 'Always Seb causing problems.'

Seb pulled a face. 'You're the one we had to drop off in this fancy hotel!'

'Your comebacks are getting better.' She smiled. 'Well done.'

'Thank you.' Seb bowed.

Hannah chuckled. 'What are you like?!'

They left the hotel, got back into the car and made their way into the city centre. They passed immaculate parks and quirky metal monuments, high-rise buildings and huge street crossings. It wasn't long before the car stopped again, this time outside the Tokyo Tower.

Hannah stepped out of the Mercedes and on to the pavement so that Seb could shuffle out. 'You're staying in there?' she asked.

'Not exactly,' said Seb. 'But the building next to it. Tokyo Tower is actually a broadcasting tower, which is why my dad's work put us so close.'

Hannah craned her neck to look all the way up to the top. She shielded her eyes from the sun and smiled. 'It's kind of like the Eiffel Tower.'

'But red and white!'

She laughed. 'I don't know who'd be more annoyed at me for saying that – the Japanese or the French.'

'We should go, once we've found the medal.'

'To here or Paris?'

'Here!' Seb laughed.

They followed Hannah's parents to the hotel across the road.

'We can do all kinds of things once we've finished,' said Hannah.

'Let me guess. Have you made a list?'

'Well . . . there is a really cool museum I want to go to,' she confessed, 'but you don't have to come.'

'Are you kidding? I'd love to! Although, good luck convincing Maria to go to something other than sports.'

Hannah shook her head. 'Not a problem. There is a sports section with her name on it!'

CHAPTER 20
JAMES BOND STYLE

Hannah and Maria were already at the upper-level sushi bar at twelve thirty. They sat slurping smoothies, courtesy of Maria's special pass, swinging their legs off their stools. Maria hauled a large backpack up on to the seat next to her and opened it up.

'I borrowed this from my sister. Have you got your kit?'

Hannah unbuckled her satchel and showed her neatly folded US tracksuit to Maria. 'Although I really don't want to wear the jacket today. It's boiling!' It was one of the hottest days in recorded history... probably. Hannah could feel the sweat dripping from her forehead. While Maria zipped up her backpack, Hannah had her eyes on the stadium entrance. She checked her watch for the third time that morning and tapped her feet against the table leg. 'Seb should be here by now, right?'

'He'll be here soon.'

Hannah picked up her phone. 'Should I send him a text?' She found his contact and began to type. *Hey, Seb?*

'Hi!' Hannah turned around to see a sweaty Seb behind them, trying to catch his breath. 'Sorry I'm late.'

Maria pulled up a stool. 'Don't worry. Grab a seat.'

He joined the others at the table and sighed. 'Wow ...' He buried his face into his palms.

'What's wrong?' asked Hannah.

'Oh, it's nothing too serious ...'

Maria looked him in the eyes. '*Too* serious?'

'Well ... it's just ... I got a message last night from an unknown number.'

Hannah studied Seb more closely. 'What did it say?'

'*Stop investigating the medal theft. It's dangerous.*'

Hannah's throat tightened. That *was* serious.

Maria leaned across the table. 'Seb, was that a threat?'

He shrugged. 'I assume so ...'

'Do we tell someone about this?' she asked.

'We could tell the police?' Hannah shifted uncomfortably. 'Although, then they would find out we've been snooping around. We wouldn't be allowed to keep investigating!' She shook her head. 'No, it's a stupid idea. They wouldn't be able to do anything with an unknown number anyway.' Hannah fought the urge to chew her nails as panic rose in her chest. 'Who do you think sent it?'

Seb's eyes darted around. 'I don't know. The thief?'

'It's likely, but we shouldn't panic.' Hannah said, though all she felt was panic.

'Yeah,' Maria added. 'We can find the thief before he does anything to us.'

'That wasn't as reassuring out loud as it probably was in your head,' whispered Hannah.

Seb managed a small smile. 'No, it's fine.' He sat up straight. 'But Maria's right. We need to catch whoever this person is off guard.'

'But how do we do that if they already know what we're doing?'

'We could pretend to give up?' he said.

'But . . .' Hannah looked around the busy concourse. 'What if they can see us now? What if they're following us?' she whispered. 'They'll know we're still looking!'

'We'll have to go undercover, James Bond style,' Seb said. 'You know, hoods up, heads down, hide in big crowds, wait until corridors are empty.'

Hannah realized she was biting her nails again and pulled her hand away. 'You think that'll work?'

'I don't know,' said Seb. 'But what else can we do? Stop looking?'

Hannah knew that was the safest thing to do. She didn't want to put her friends at risk. Whoever sent the threat sounded serious.

'Maybe we should stop . . .' she muttered.

Maria frowned. 'Damn, you really think so?'

'Well, yeah.' Hannah sighed. 'Keeping you safe is more important than finding a medal.'

'I didn't think of you as a quitter,' Maria sighed.

'I'm not quitting! We're being *forced* to finish.'

Seb slammed his fist on to the table. 'Well, I'm not being forced to do anything! I'm not taking orders from a bad guy!'

'Or girl!' Maria rolled her eyes.

Seb looked at Hannah. 'What does your mum do when she meets bad people in her work? Does she do what they say? Or does she do what she believes is right?'

Seb had a point. Her mum was always telling her, '*Hannah, you must do what you think is right. Not what other people tell you is right!*'

'Okay, if you're sure.' Hannah reached for her notebook. 'We'll keep going.'

The others grinned. 'Yes!' they said in unison.

'But if Seb gets another threat, we're calling it off.'

Seb nodded. 'Deal.'

'And we need to keep an eye out for anyone around us,' Hannah added. 'Suspect everyone.'

'We'd better get to work!' said Maria.

'Okay . . .' Hannah turned to their list of suspects and began to think. 'Whoever sent the text knows that we're on the case, and there are two people who definitely know.'

'Fred from the food hall?' Maria said.

Hannah twiddled her pen. 'I'm not saying he definitely sent it, but he could be an accomplice. Maybe he told Marcus about us. Or even Jesse.'

'It's not Jess—' Maria started, but Hannah interjected. 'I know, I know, but he's still on our suspects list.'

'Or Ren.' The girls turned to Seb. 'He knows we're looking for the medal. Maybe he was warning us about something.'

Hannah took a long slurp from her smoothie. 'He could be, but Ren wouldn't message you from an unknown number, would he?'

'I've just remembered!' Maria flapped her hands. 'I gave Marcus your number!'

Hannah frowned. 'Didn't he screw up the paper?'

'Maybe he went back for it.'

Hannah could sense a flicker of panic in Seb. 'Why

don't we focus on finding the medal,' she said, standing up and slinging her satchel over her shoulder. 'We're not making any progress with finding the thief, or Jesse himself, so let's try to retrace the steps again.'

'Yeah!' Seb stood up. 'We need to find out where Jesse went right after the ceremony.' He tucked his stool under the table. 'Fred said he thought Jesse had his medal at the dinner, but I haven't seen a single photo of him wearing it.'

'Maybe that's because it was in his pocket.'

Hannah turned to Maria. 'That's a bit weird, though, isn't it? Surely he'd wear it for some photos and *then* put it away in his pocket.'

Maria nodded. 'And Fred must have seen Jesse put the medal in there, to know where it was.'

'Do you think Fred lied to us?' Seb asked.

'He could have done.' Hannah opened up her phone's web browser and searched for pictures. She scrolled through hundreds of images – Maria and Seb were right. There was no sign of Jesse's medal. 'Do you think Fred was trying to throw us off?' she said.

'Probably.' Seb shrugged.

'Okay . . .' She swapped her phone for her notebook. 'I'll add him to the suspect list.' She drew an arrow between Marcus and Fred. 'Something tells me that they're connected.'

Maria leaned closer. 'What makes you say that?'

'I have no idea . . . but what I do know is that we need to find out, once and for all, where Jesse went after the ceremony.'

'How?' asked Maria. 'We couldn't find any information before.'

'But now we have a secret weapon.'

'What?'

'Ren.'

Maria nodded. 'Yeah, but it's Onishi we really need. He's the one with the footage.'

'And anyway,' said Seb. 'Doesn't he think we're competing today?'

'Oh yeah . . .' Hannah had forgotten about their lie.

'Wait – the gymnastics finishes at one o'clock,' Maria said. Hannah smiled – Maria's knowledge of the events was amazing. 'So we can ask him after that. It's less than half an hour.'

Hannah took a sip of her sweet berry smoothie. 'So, what do we do now?'

Maria grinned. 'Watch some sport, of course!'

'Is there nothing else we can do?' Hannah sighed.

Maria laughed. 'I'm afraid not.'

CHAPTER 21
INCOMING

The trio set off in the direction of the stands.

'All my family's here,' said Maria, 'so I don't have any spare passes, sorry.'

Seb looked at his day pass. 'I'm in Block C today, but there's no point going all the way over there. I'll just wait here on the concourse until one o'clock.'

'By yourself?' Maria said.

'My dad is all the way over in Block G,' said Hannah. 'I'll wait with Seb. I've seen loads of stuff this morning anyway.'

There was a huge roar from the stands and Maria ran over to the entrance to see what was happening.

'Yes!' She jumped up and down. 'She did it!'

'An American?' asked Hannah.

'Anita Grey just took the lead in the javelin!'

Hannah looked up at a nearby TV screen to see the replay, Grey's javelin looping up high into the air.

'Ah!' Maria peered down at them from the top of the stairs. 'I can see Sakura. Shall I try to speak to her?'

'Yes!' Hannah was desperate to make progress, and speaking to Sakura was a chance to do something. 'Ask her if she's seen Onishi today.'

'But I thought we were going to ask Ren?'

'It won't hurt to ask someone else. For all we know, Onishi could be down there.' She pointed to the underground level.

Maria shrugged. 'We'd still have to wait until one o'clock to see him. He thinks we're competing.'

'Yes, but . . .' Hannah inched closer so she didn't have to shout up at her friend. 'We can do something now. We might not even be able to get hold of Ren. We need to keep our options open!'

'All right, then.' Maria laughed. 'A minute ago, you wanted us to stop!'

'Yeah, and then we decided to carry on. If you're okay with that?'

Maria gave a very definite nod. 'We've got to find this medal for Jesse.' She spun on her heel and strode off.

Hannah watched as Maria made her way past the

volunteers and into the stand. Over her shoulder she heard Seb gasp.

'Epic! They bring back the javelins on mini cars. Have you seen it?'

Hannah joined Seb watching the TV screen and giggled as a tiny remote-controlled pick-up truck raced back to the officials with a javelin on its roof. 'Aw, that's cute.'

Hannah turned back to see Maria's progress and grimaced. It looked as if Maria had been collared by her parents and was sitting sandwiched next to her sister.

Hannah couldn't help but smile as Isabella climbed up on to her seat and shouted out to the American athlete. Maria swiftly picked her up and bounced her on her knee.

The four Campbells leaped into the air as the tannoy announced, '*New Games record for Anita Grey!*'

Beside her, Seb raised Hannah's arm into the air and

jumped up and down. 'USA! USA!'

It was the loudest chant in the stadium as Anita's throw propelled her into the final. Hannah saw Maria sneaking away to find Sakura while her family were distracted by Grey's lap of honour.

'Can you tell what she's saying?' asked Seb.

'How good do you think my eyesight is?'

'If it's as good as your note-taking, exceptional.'

Hannah didn't have to wait long for Maria to report back.

'So . . .' Maria began. 'Sakura hasn't seen Onishi this morning, but she says he's been here every day.'

Hannah scratched her face. 'What's the time?'

Maria checked her watch. 'Twelve forty-five.'

'We don't have long, then. You go and watch more with your family, and meet back here at one o'clock?'

Maria clapped her hands. 'Sounds good!'

Hannah grinned when Maria came down the stairs at 12.57 p.m.

'I told Mom and Dad we were going to have lunch together,' Maria said.

'Great – I'm starving!' Seb said. 'I saw a bento stall outside the stadium?'

Hannah rolled her eyes. 'All you ever think about is food! Come on, then. We have a couple of minutes anyway...'

They made their way out of the stadium and over to a bench beside the bento food cart. While Maria used her pass to get them a bento box each, Hannah sat down on the bench and turned to Seb.

'You ready?'

'Can I eat first?'

'Really, Seb?!'

'Ha, no, but you should have seen your face.' Seb grinned. 'Just let me get my phone out!'

Seb dialled Ren's number and held the phone to his ear.

'Is he calling?' asked Maria, wandering over with their lunch. Hannah nodded.

Seb turned on speaker-phone mode.

'Hiya!' answered Ren. 'How was the competition?'

'Ah, pretty good, Ren, thank you.' He lowered his voice and brought the phone to his mouth. 'Hey, you know that we're looking for the medal?'

'Yes.'

Seb explained to Ren why the friends needed to get hold of his dad's footage. 'Do you think you can help?'

'Of course!' Ren replied. 'This would make a great

story for the documentary!'

Seb high-fived the girls before calmly responding, 'You're a star, thank you.'

'Every lunchtime, my dad films his morning recap. He should be there now,' Ren explained. 'Try the media storeroom. He will be setting up his equipment in there.'

'Thank you!'

'You are welcome, but be quick. He is there only for a little bit today. He has to film the end of the parade.'

Hannah mouthed to Seb. *'Ask where the storeroom is!'*

Seb nodded and asked Ren.

'It is on the underground level. You cannot go through the media entrance, so you will have to sneak through the conference room – it links the two corridors.'

'Hold on a second. Let me just write this down.' He turned to Hannah, who was already scribbling frantically. 'Actually, never mind, keep going.'

'Once you're through the conference room—'

Hannah heard a muffled voice in the background of the call.

'Sorry! It is my brother. We have to leave for the parade. We are helping to prepare.'

There were more muffled sounds and the call went dead.

'We need to know how to get to the storeroom!' said Hannah.

'What could I do?' argued Seb. 'He had to go.'

'Okay.' Maria held out her hands. 'Come on, you two. We could send him a text?'

Seb started typing into his phone as the others looked over his shoulder: *Hey, Ren, do you have time to tell us the way to the storeroom?*

The three of them sat and waited. Hannah willed three little dots to appear to indicate that Ren was typing, but . . . nothing.

'He hasn't even opened it,' said Seb.

'Try ringing him again!' said Hannah.

He dialled Ren's number.

. . .

. . .

. . .

Nothing.

Hannah slumped on the bench and growled. 'Ugh!'

'It's a long shot, but we could try to ring Onishi,' Maria suggested. 'He seemed pretty awesome. We could just ask him directly about the footage?'

Seb shrugged as a loud cheer came from within the stadium. 'Let's do it. Ren said to be quick, so we need to find him fast.'

Hannah searched online for Onishi Shig's contact details, or a website, but nothing came up. She grimaced. 'All I can see are loads of bad articles.'

Seb peered over. 'Like what?'

'It looks like he does a lot of stuff for the prime minister, but the other politicians don't like him.' She scrolled through the headlines that were in English, and read out a few of the words: '*"Dinosaur"*, *"Stubborn"*, *"Selfish"*.' She turned to the others. 'But he didn't seem like that at all?' She shook her head. 'My mum says that mean people attack those they are jealous of.'

'In that case –' Seb cringed – 'they must be very jealous, because what they're saying is *bad*.'

There was a buzz from Seb's phone and he flipped it over to check the message.

'Is that Ren?' asked Maria.

He shook his head.

'Another threat?' Hannah guessed.

Seb gulped and nodded. 'The same as last time.'

As Hannah reached over to take a look, the ringer blared out. Startled, Seb dropped the phone on to the bench and they all peered down at it. Across the screen it read in bold INCOMING CALL (JAPAN).

CHAPTER 22
MIME ARTISTS

Seb fumbled for his phone. 'What should I do?' he asked, the ringer still blaring out.

Hannah noticed heads turning in their direction. 'Answer it!' she whispered. 'People are staring.' Her entire body went suddenly cold as she wondered if the thief was watching them – while he called them. It was like something out of a movie.

Seb swiped across and the ringer fell silent. The girls leaned in and Seb slowly brought the phone to his ear.

'Hello?'

Hannah heard a thick German accent on the other end. '*Sebastian, geht es dir gut?*'

Seb gave an enormous sigh. 'Oh, Dad, hi!'

His dad let out a deep chuckle. 'Who did you think I was?'

'I don't know. I forgot to save your Japanese phone number!'

Hannah sat back and let the pair of them speak. She looked at Maria and pretended to wipe sweat from her forehead.

Maria mimed her reply, pointing to Hannah and mouthing, '*You.*' She tapped her head, then gestured to Seb, finally circling her eyes with her fingers, as if she was playing charades.

Hannah tilted her head to the side. 'What?'

Maria got on to her tiptoes and crept around the bench.

'What?' Hannah looked confused.

Maria sneaked her hand into Seb's pocket.

'Okay, I have no idea what that means!' Hannah said, screwing up her face.

Maria sighed. 'Did you think the call was going to be the thief?'

'Oh, that's what you meant!'

'It was good – you just couldn't understand it!'

Hannah laughed. 'You could have mimed a medal!'

Seb put his phone back into his pocket and turned to each of the girls. 'You would make terrible mime artists.'

Hannah stuck out her tongue. 'See!'

'Anyway, my dad wants to meet me at the media centre.'

'That's not a bad idea,' said Hannah. 'There'll be loads of footage of Jesse, so maybe we don't need Onishi's after all. We should be safe there too, right?'

'Exactly,' he said.

'How do we get there?'

'It's about a ten-minute walk to the other side of the park.' Hannah picked up her satchel. 'Then let's get going.'

'One more thing . . .' said Seb.

She turned around. 'Yeah?'

Seb shuffled his feet. 'I said I'd spend some time with my dad.'

'Yeah, that's cool. We're doing that.'

'No.' He dropped his bag down on the bench. 'I mean quality time . . . I don't see my dad very often, and I think sometimes he feels bad.'

Hannah felt her stomach twist. 'Oh, I didn't know.' She flashed him a smile. 'Go and see your dad, and Maria and I can take care of the footage.'

'But I want to keep investigating.' He shrugged. 'Aside from the threats, it's been fun.'

'You will be helping the investigation!'

'How?'

'While you distract your dad, we can speak to other media crews.'

Seb slowly nodded. 'Sure that's okay?'

Maria rested her hand on his shoulder. 'Yeah, if anything, you've been slowing us down.'

'Oi!' He gave her a playful nudge.

Hannah waved them along. 'Come on. Let's go.'

After precisely twelve minutes, the trio arrived at the media centre – a huge white cube with perfectly symmetrical windows. It looked like the kind of thing that would win architecture awards, thought Hannah.

Seb's dad was waiting to greet them by the front entrance. He looked different to the last two times Hannah had seen him. His Afro hair was neatly combed and his navy suit matched the mini microphone on his lapel. He waved to the trio and smiled.

The girls followed Seb to the door and his dad opened his arms.

'Don't worry –' he beamed as Seb gave him a hug – 'the mic isn't on.' He gave Hannah and Maria a fist bump. 'You can say what you like.'

'It's nice to properly meet you,' Hannah said, smiling. Looking at his dad, she could see where Seb's energy came from.

'Here, take these!' He handed them a visitor badge each. 'I will show you around.'

Hannah clipped her badge to her crimson tea dress and hurried through the tall double doors.

From the outside, the media centre looked like it was a building for lab-tech scientists. But on the inside, it was filled with colour and interesting displays. Projected on to the walls was a selection of landscapes, from the busy streets of Tokyo to the tranquil Aogashima Island. There was even a corner of the room dedicated to art from the local schools. Seb's dad stopped at a bridge in the middle of the room over a ginormous koi pond.

'The path to your left takes you to the interview rooms. The path to your right takes you to the editing rooms.'

Seb followed the fish with his eyes. 'I always wondered how they got in here?' he whispered to himself.

'Hey! Are you listening, Seb?'

He gave his dad a grin. 'Yeahhh.'

Seb's dad put an arm on his shoulder. 'Let me show you the coolest part. It is straight ahead.' He led the friends straight over the bridge and down what seemed to be the world's longest escalator. 'This is the hangout room, where all the broadcasters take their breaks and rehearse their ideas.'

'What, like actors?' said Hannah, jumping off when they reached the bottom.

'Yes.' Seb's dad led them through two giant wooden doors. 'You can practise with us, if you like. Seb always likes to.'

'Johann!' a voice called out.

Seb's dad waved to one of his colleagues. 'Max! Hi!' He walked everyone over to a circle of beanbags and sofas. 'Let me introduce you to Hannah and Maria. They are friends of Sebastian.'

'Then you're friends of mine. Johann and I – and Sebastian – go way back.'

Hannah shook Max's outstretched hand. 'So you've worked with Seb's dad before?'

Max gave him a nudge and winked. 'Oh, many, many times! Longer than I care to remember.' He had a German accent just like Seb's dad's, only a little softer. He sank into a corduroy beanbag and smiled. 'I've been his cameraman for fifteen years.'

'I bet you have a lot of footage,' she said, taking a seat opposite him.

'Years' worth!'

Seb's dad turned to his son. 'Will you help me rehearse?'

Seb nodded.

'We won't be long,' his dad said to Maria and Hannah.

'See ya later!' Hannah waved.

While Seb and his dad wandered off, Maria sat down beside Hannah.

'Where was I?' Max chuckled. 'Oh yes, too much footage!'

Hannah felt a sneaky tap on her back from Maria. 'Where does it all go?' she asked.

'Oh, I don't know.' He rubbed his chin. 'The current stuff is sent to the producers, and anything old is in the archives.' He levelled a gaze at the two of them. 'Why do you ask? Do you want something?'

Hannah gave an awkward laugh. 'Ha ha, good one.'

Max's face remained stern. He rested his hands on his knees and whispered, 'I'm watching you three.'

Hannah felt her anxiety pooling in her stomach.

He rose out of the beanbag and reached across a table to the side.

'What's happening?' whispered Maria to Hannah in a panicked voice.

Max slid something from the table top and hid it under his blazer. Hannah scanned the room in search of Seb. All she could see was a sea of burgundy corduroy.

'This should satisfy you . . .' Max jeered. He sat back down and held out his palm, revealing some earphones. His face broke into a grin. 'So let me show you our best footage!'

Hannah laughed, relieved, and took the headphones.

'Oh jeez!' squealed Maria. 'I was so scared!'

'I shouldn't have been so cruel, but the looks on your faces were priceless.' Max rested his laptop on the table and beckoned to Hannah and Maria. 'I will put it here so we can all see it.' He pointed to the side of the laptop. 'You can plug the earphones in there.'

The girls stood up and Hannah slotted the earphone jack into the hole and handed one of the buds to Maria. She watched the screen as Max signed in and searched through a labyrinth of files. In the corner, an email notification popped up: *Jesse interview. MUST WATCH!*

CHAPTER 23
EDNA

'Sorry.' Max clicked on the email. 'I need to watch this.'

'Oh.' Hannah unplugged the earphones.

'Oh no, you can watch too! It probably is not that long. He has not been very chatty with interviews since his medal was stolen.'

Hannah turned to Maria and resisted the urge to jump. Maria's eyes were practically bulging with excitement.

'Johann!' Max had somehow managed to spot his colleague and waved him over.

Seb and his dad hurried back and everybody gathered round the laptop.

'What's all this?' asked Seb's dad.

Max pressed play on the video. 'We're about to find out.'

The video was an interview with Jesse outside the

US block in the athletes' village. Hannah dived into her satchel for her notebook. As she pulled out the pad and a pen, the interviewer started with the usual pleasantries.

'Hey, Jesse, thanks for speaking to me. So sorry about the medal . . . Is there any news about it? Any leads?'

Hannah clicked her pen and listened as Jesse spoke. 'No, nothing at all. So we've raised the reward to sixty thousand dollars. I'll do anything to get it back. My medals mean the world to me. They represent so much hard work and sacrifice.'

'You must be heartbroken! Do you remember where you last saw it?'

Jesse shook his head. 'I just keep replaying the evening over and over again, but I can't really remember.'

'Surely you must remember something?'

'I told you, I don't!' He buried his head in his hands. 'All I know is that I zipped it in my pocket at some point.'

'When did you put it in there?'

'I told you, I dunno. After the ceremony? On the bus?'

The interviewer leaned in. 'So, it could have been taken anywhere between the ceremony and when you woke up the next day.'

'Not exactly,' said Jesse. 'It wasn't in my pocket at the

dinner that evening, but I just assumed that I'd left it in my bag at my apartment.'

'You didn't think, Oh, I must bring my medal with me?'

'I thought it was in my pocket!' he snapped.

'But then you thought it was in your bag?'

'When I realized it wasn't in my pocket at dinner, I just assumed that I'd put it in my bag! My first thought wasn't, Oh, somebody must have stolen it!'

Maria whispered to Hannah, 'This interviewer is terrible! He's not listening to Jesse at all!'

'Have the police made much progress?' the interviewer asked.

'They give me regular updates.'

'How close to finding the medal are they?'

'Not close at all – I've already said that.'

'Well, when you have some news, you know where to come.' The interviewer turned to the camera. *'There's the latest on Marks's missing medal. Was it cunning or carelessness?'*

'I can't believe he said that!' Maria sat down on the table. 'Right in front of Jesse!'

'He was a bit rude,' said Seb. He spun around. 'What do you think, Dad?'

His dad smiled. 'I think Max and I could do a better job. But it's so hard to get an interview with him.'

'We *are* trying!' Max packed his laptop into a case and waved to a woman on the other side of the room. 'I'll speak to Erin and see if we can make a piece about the reward doubling for the evening show.' He turned to the girls. 'Erin is head of production. She makes all the decisions.'

Hannah watched Erin weave through the stray chairs and beanbags. She was a little older-looking than her mum, and a little shorter too. With her cropped black hair and glasses, Erin reminded Hannah of Edna Mode from *The Incredibles*.

'Ah, Sebastian!' She looked at Hannah and Maria. '*Wer sind deine Freundinnen?*'

Seb stood next to the girls. 'This is Hannah and Maria. We all met at the athletics the other day.'

'It is nice to meet you both.' Erin smiled, then turned to the two men. 'Okay, you two, why do you want me?'

Max explained how they wanted to do a special report on Jesse, with the new information they'd found. Hannah thought it was kind they were speaking in English rather than switching to German. It made her wish she was better at other languages.

'Of course you can!' Erin rolled her eyes. 'You don't have to ask me that.'

'When will the team in Berlin need it by?' Seb's dad asked.

'About one hour.'

'Oh . . .' He frowned. 'That soon?'

'Sorry, but they are very busy.' She started to make her way back through the beanbag maze, talking over her shoulder. 'I am here until two o'clock, then I go to the pentathlon.'

'Okay.' Seb's dad turned to him and sighed. 'I'm sorry, I'm going to have to work – maybe you could come back later?'

'That's okay.' Seb nodded. 'When you finish tonight, we can stop for cookies like we did last summer at the Women's World Cup.'

'Oh yes!' His dad chuckled. 'Cookie Fridays. Perfect!'

'We'll go over to the stadium, then,' Seb said.

Hannah gritted her teeth. It looked like they weren't going to see Max's footage after all. They'd have to go back to plan A: find Onishi.

'Is that okay?' said Seb's dad. 'I can try to finish early if you like.' Then he pretended to whisper, 'Max won't mind clearing up for me.'

'I will!'

Seb laughed. 'I'll see you at five. Then we can get

dinner *and* cookies on the way home.'

'I like your thinking.' Seb's dad held out his fist to Hannah and Maria. 'It was nice of you to come along. Hopefully I'll see you more tomorrow.'

With a final round of fist bumps, Hannah, Seb and Maria left the white cube to head back to the stadium.

As they emerged into the sweltering heat, Hannah could feel her sweat mixing with the suncream she'd put on that morning. She shuddered at the feeling of it.

'You all right?' said Seb.

She put on a smile. 'I'm more of a cold-weather person.'

'At least you're not competing in it!'

He was right. Not that she was good enough at any sports to be a professional! She liked watching it, but she'd prefer to be reading or writing than running around getting sweaty. Hannah thought back to her notebook and the latest information that could help their investigation.

'Did you hear what Jesse said in that interview?' she asked her friends.

'About not having his medal at the dinner?' Seb asked.

'Yeah . . .'

'It must mean that it was stolen before then.'

They joined the top of the spectators' path.

'Does that mean that Machi didn't do it?' Maria asked.

Hannah thought for a moment. 'She wasn't at the stadium on the day of the medal ceremony, and Fred said she was at the dinner.'

'So, you think she was setting up her equipment?' Maria asked.

'Surely not all day?'

'She could have arrived early in order to steal the medal,' Maria said.

Seb shook his head. 'It would've been impossible to sneak around. You saw how much stuff Dad and Max had.'

'Could she have left it somewhere?' Hannah asked.

'Not unless she wanted that to be stolen too.' He shrugged.

They passed the velodrome gymnastics arena as a gaggle of fans ran in the opposite direction.

'We need that footage more than ever,' said Hannah.

Seb shrugged. 'I guess.'

'Think about it!' she said. 'The medal could only have been stolen in three places: in the stadium, on the bus, or in Jesse's apartment, assuming he went back there before the dinner.'

'Why couldn't it have been stolen when he was walking through the village?'

'It's possible,' Hannah said, 'but unlikely. I can't imagine the thief unzipping Jesse's pocket and taking the medal without him noticing.'

'But why is the footage even more important now?' asked Maria.

'Because, if it proves that nobody stole the medal in the stadium, then it was either stolen by someone on his bus, which is bound to have CCTV, or someone in his apartment.'

'Marcus!' Maria cried.

Hannah raised her eyebrows and nodded. 'Maybe Marcus.'

CHAPTER 24
BINGO

'Any messages from Ren?' Hannah asked as they went through the stadium's security checks.

He pulled out his phone. 'Nothing.'

'Nothing at all?'

Seb passed her the phone and winked. 'You want to check for yourself?'

'It's okay, I trust you.' She smiled. 'I just thought that he would've replied by now.'

'Looks like we've gotta find the storeroom ourselves,' Maria said.

'Any ideas on how to get there?' asked Seb.

'You heard Ren. We've gotta go to the underground level.'

Hannah shook her head. 'But how do we get into the conference room?'

Seb clutched the straps on his backpack. 'Easy.'

Hannah laughed. 'You remember the last time we tried, don't you?'

'Yeah, but . . .' Seb pulled the visitor badge from his pocket. 'You know these things my dad gave each of us?'

'Yeah?'

'They give us access to all the media sections.'

'So . . .' Hannah grinned. 'We can go anywhere?'

'Only for today, but yes.'

'Awesome!' Maria patted Seb on the back. 'I knew you were good for something!'

'Even though these passes get us into the media section,' Hannah said, 'I think we should still get there through the athletes' section. We haven't got time to look around and we know the guards let us into the athlete bit.'

Seb nodded. 'I'm not going to argue with that, and my dad hasn't taken me to the stadium media section yet, so I don't know my way around it.'

The trio found the nearest toilets and slipped into their athlete kit. Just like yesterday, the volunteer in the stands hurried them through to the athlete. They then went down the lift and made their way through the athlete corridor.

'Here we go!' Seb said as the conference room door

appeared up ahead. He approached the volunteer on the door. The man simply nodded and waved them through.

The conference room was completely empty. Not a soul to be seen, nor a single camera. Only rows of chairs and a crate of water bottles.

Seb closed the door behind him. 'Look at this!' He pointed to the microphones lined up along the panellists' table at the front. 'Imagine how many people you can talk to at once.'

'We haven't got time for guessing!' said Maria.

He jumped up on to the platform. 'But if you had to . . .'

Maria pushed up her glasses. 'I dunno, fifty?'

'Only fifty?'

'If we don't hurry, then someone else will find the medal and they'll be sitting here instead of you,' Maria teased. 'You wouldn't want that, would you?'

Seb immediately jumped down. 'Absolutely not!'

Hannah grimaced. In her eyes there was only one thing worse than giving up, and that was being beaten. She opened the door to the media corridor and turned to the others.

'Okay, left or right?'

The three of them took a peek. The space was identical to the athletes' section with its grey walls and blue doors.

'Right must lead to the track,' said Seb.

Maria stepped out. 'So, let's go left.'

Seb slipped out into the corridor and the girls followed. It wasn't long before Seb came to a stop.

'Bingo. Hello, Onishi.'

Hannah looked up and saw a narrow black door labelled STOREROOM.

'We found it!' She pumped her fist. 'We actually found it.'

Seb opened the door and revealed a room full of lockers. Their dark red metal stretched across all four walls, leaving just enough room for a square table in the middle.

Just as Hannah stepped inside, a lone camerawoman collected her things and left the trio alone.

Hannah frowned. 'I thought there'd be more people setting up in here. A chance to see what everyone's working on.'

All was silent except for the whirring air-conditioning unit.

'Shoot, looks like Onishi already left,' said Maria.

'I had a feeling he would have,' Hannah said sulkily.

Maria walked up to a row of lockers. 'We may not have found *him*, but his stuff might be in here . . .'

Hannah looked around for security cameras. 'We can't steal it!'

Maria rattled a locker. 'Damn it! They're locked.'

A little relieved, Hannah opened the storeroom door. 'Can we leave before someone sees us looking suspicious? We could go back to the media centre and see if anyone has any footage there?'

Maria and Seb trailed out, muttering to each other.

'This is impossible.'

'Stupid thief.'

Hannah pulled the door open with a swing and it slipped from her hand. There was a huge crash as it hit the wall and she winced, scurrying back inside to see the damage she'd caused. The contents of the bin were littered across the floor.

'Oh no!'

Seb and Maria dived to the floor and quickly swept up the mess. Hannah turned the bin the right way up but heard a thump at the bottom.

'God, that's heavy!' she huffed.

'What's in it?' asked Maria.

Hannah peered inside. It

was a white travel case with gold metal running right the way around it. Wait . . . she'd seen this case before. Somewhere in the stadium. When she was in the stands.

A lightbulb pinged on in her head. 'It's Machi's case!'

Seb jumped to his feet. 'What?'

'The one we saw her assistant carrying yesterday!' Hannah explained.

'How can you tell? There must be loads like it!'

Hannah had never been so sure of anything in her life. 'I know it is! It's exactly the same size and shape . . . Even the gold star on the side is the same!'

'But why is it in the bin?' Maria reached in and pulled the case out. 'We gotta open this!' She laid the case on the table and unclipped the locks.

'Hold on.' Hannah slammed her hand on the case. 'We don't know what's inside!'

'Seriously?' Maria laughed.

'It could be dangerous!' said Hannah. 'If Machi *is* the thief, what else could she be capable of?'

'Are you suggesting murder?' Maria asked.

'I don't know!'

'Whatever it is,' said Seb calmly, 'it must have passed stadium security.'

239

'Yeah,' Maria assured Hannah. 'It's probably just broken kit . . . or something she's hiding?'

'Like a medal!' said Seb.

Hannah nodded. 'Or other people's footage?'

Seb lifted the lid of the case.

It wasn't footage that was inside. Or a medal. Or broken equipment, or books, or anything. It was completely empty.

Hannah shook her head. 'What?! Why is there nothing inside?'

'This doesn't make sense.' Maria frowned, pushing up her glasses. 'Why would Machi put a perfect case in the bin?'

Hannah stared into the empty case. 'Whatever she's done, it only makes me more suspicious of her.'

'It's a long shot,' Maria suggested, 'but we could take it to her and ask.'

'But if she's done something illegal, she isn't going to tell us,' Hannah said.

'If we catch her off—'

The door opened, interrupting Maria, and a frantic teenager ran over to one of the lockers. She unlocked it and scrambled around inside before rushing back into the corridor empty-handed.

'I bet she's an intern.' Seb chuckled. He turned to Maria. 'What were you saying?'

Maria refastened the clasps on the white case. 'If she doesn't tell us why it was in the bin, then we can threaten to hand the case to the police.'

'But why would she tell us?' said Hannah. 'If she's the one threatening Seb, god knows what she'll do if she finds out we have the case.'

'So where does that leave us?'

Hannah leaned against the table, biting her nails subconsciously. What would make Machi confess?

'We need to work out how Machi stole the medal,' Hannah said. 'Piece it all together.'

Seb laughed. 'How on earth are we going to do that?'

'By using the notes I made earlier.' Hannah opened her notebook and rested it on the table. 'We know that Sakura didn't see Machi at the stadium, so if we get Onishi's footage of Jesse, we can prove that it wasn't stolen there.'

'Which means it was stolen in the village, probably by Machi!' Maria exclaimed.

Hannah turned to Maria. 'Exactly, which means that it must have been stolen at the dinner, after all!'

Maria frowned. 'But how? Fred said it was so busy,

there would have been loads of witnesses.'

Hannah nodded. 'Machi must have been really close to him at one point.'

'I think I know!' Seb suddenly said.

'If she put the microphone on him, he would've taken his jacket off . . . The microphone goes under your top –' Seb gasped – 'and they put the microphone pack in your pocket!'

Hannah felt like her brain had exploded. 'I bet she took it there and then!'

'Exactly!' Seb squeaked. 'He wouldn't have noticed, because the packs probably weigh the same as the medals.'

Hannah snapped her notebook shut. 'And that's why Jesse thought he'd left it back at the apartment! Because it went missing before the dinner even began!'

Maria grabbed the case by the handle. 'I bet she put the medal in here! And then binned it in case it could link her to the theft!'

Hannah hurried to the door. 'We need to get Onishi's footage now! It'll show that the medal wasn't stolen in the Sportpark, and the white case proves that Machi probably stole it.'

'Do you think Onishi's at the parade?' asked Seb.

'He must be. Ren said so – and my guess is that Machi

is too.' Hannah turned the door handle and spun round. 'Let's go!'

The trio quietly left the storeroom, with Maria carrying the case, and headed towards the conference room. Hannah followed the sound of cheering fans and hurried down the corridor. As she reached the conference room, she looked up at the volunteer guarding the door.

'Accreditation, please.'

As Hannah lifted up her visitor badge, she spotted the tunnel to the track and saw some presenters rehearsing their lines . . . including a man in a pinstripe suit. She let go of her badge.

'No way!'

'What?' said Maria.

'It's Onishi!'

Seb wasted no time, running up to the crew. 'Mr Shig!' he said in his New Yorker accent.

The director extended a hand and grinned. 'Cam! How are you? Please call me Shig.'

'We're great, thanks!' Seb waved over his fellow 'gymnasts'.

'Good!' Onishi smiled. 'What are you doing now?'

'We're seeing what it's like behind the scenes. Ever since Ren told us about your work, we've been desperate to see what you've been working on.'

Onishi crouched down beside the crew's pile of stuff. 'You should have said. I'll ask my assistant to show you.' He waved to a girl with a briefcase. 'Cari!'

A tall, crimson-haired girl who looked somehow familiar came running over. '*Hai?*'

'Show these three our behind-the-scenes footage of the long jump.' Onishi turned back to the trio. 'It's our best work yet!'

Seb forced a smile. 'I don't suppose you have any of Jesse?'

'I am afraid not. The police have it for their investigation.'

Hannah gritted her teeth. Of course they did. What were they going to do now?! She watched the girl close her laptop and slot it back into her briefcase.

Another lady with a headset walked up to Onishi and straightened his tie. 'You're on in ten. Let's go.'

'Oh, sorry.' He bowed to the friends. 'That's my ten-minute warning – I need to talk about the documentary I'm making. I will see you later.'

'It was nice to see you!' Seb waved. He faced the girls and sighed. 'Of course the police have it! Why didn't we think of that?'

Hannah's brain whirred as they made their way out of the tunnel. 'Okay, but we still have the case.'

Maria waved it in the air.

'Good.' Hannah set off down the corridor. 'I know video proof would be better, but we still have Sakura's statement that Machi wasn't at the stadium.'

'So next stop, the parade? How are we gonna get there?' asked Maria.

'It'll say where it is on the Tokyo Games app . . . Or we could ask one of the volunteers here . . .' Hannah spun around to look for one. What she wasn't expecting was a scowling man to be sprinting towards them.

'Uh-oh . . .' she stuttered.

'Yeah?' Maria asked.

'Run!'

CHAPTER 25
NEVER MIND THE DRINKS!

The three friends tore down the corridor in the direction of the conference room. Hannah stole a glance over her shoulder at the man chasing after them.

'Why are we being chased?' yelled Maria.

'Maybe Machi had someone guarding the case?' guessed Hannah.

'Why do I have to be the one carrying it?!'

'Because you're the fastest!' said Seb.

'Oh, great!'

The corridor was becoming busier by the second. It was impossible for Hannah to see where they were going, and when she looked back, she saw the man was gaining on them.

'Where are we going?' cried Seb.

'Through the conference room and out the stadium!' Hannah yelled.

'Where is it?' Maria shouted. 'All the doors look the same!'

Hannah recognized the volunteer guarding the conference room door. 'Second door on the left!'

The three of them weaved in and out of a flurry of people with bags and suitcases. As they approached the door, Hannah took another look around. The man was getting caught up in the traffic.

'We're losing him!' she said. 'Get the volunteer to open the door!'

'I'm on it!' Maria waved her

accreditation in the air. 'Hey! Excuse me!'

The volunteer let them into the conference room and Maria dived inside.

Seb and Hannah followed, and Hannah slammed the door behind them and winced. 'Sorry,' she said, as if the volunteer could hear her.

Maria led them past a group of volunteers placing a bottle of water on each chair. She raced to the other side of the room and flung open another door.

'In there!' shouted a gravelly voice from the door behind them.

'He's close!' cried Hannah.

'Quick, do something!' Seb yelled.

Hannah turned to the volunteers setting up. 'Sorry for what I'm about to do!' She hooked her foot under a chair and kicked it with all her might. She raced away, looking behind her to see the man trip and tumble to the floor.

Maria whizzed around the corner and bolted for the foyer. As they approached the entrance, Hannah spotted a fresh batch of athletes stepping off a bus.

'Let's aim for the huddle! We'll blend in!'

Maria darted into the crowd, Hannah and Seb following, weaving their way into the middle.

'Let's follow these athletes to the prep area,' Maria

whispered as they kept low in the moving crowd. 'Then we can sneak out when Machi's guard is gone.'

Hannah stole another glance over her shoulder but couldn't see the man.

'We're coming up to the athlete prep area,' Maria whispered, 'so we've gotta stay away from the Americans.'

Seb chuckled nervously. 'More than usual?'

'It's even more important here. They all do athletics.'

Hannah nodded. 'One look at us and they'll instantly know we're fakes – they won't recognize us.'

They entered through a set of double doors and into a huge room divided into sections. In the centre was a running track, and on the perimeter were taped-off areas with mats and massage tables.

Maria sighed. 'If we weren't being hunted down by a giant working for Machi, I'd take so many photos.'

'Yeah.' Hannah looked around for any Americans. 'I'd save that for another day.'

'Psst.' Seb tilted his head to the side. 'Americans at three o'clock.'

Hannah spotted the USA's team area in the far-right corner of the room. It took up a long stretch of wall, with massage tables lined up one after another. On the floor mats, coaches were singing along to the music from a speaker, presumably waiting for the athletes to arrive.

Hannah turned her back to them. 'We need to find a space where they can't see us.'

'What about here?' Maria ducked into a side room on her left. She stuck her head back around the door. 'It's empty apart from some people in Kenya kit.'

Hannah and Seb joined her inside the room. It was packed with drinks and snacks.

'Wow!' Seb eyed up the wall of fridges. 'There's a lifetime supply of hydro drinks in here!'

'Never mind the drinks.' Maria took a seat on the sofa. 'What the hell just happened?'

'There are only two possible reasons why that man was chasing us,' said Hannah. 'Either he knows that we're not really athletes, or he doesn't want us to have the case.'

'If we'd been found out, then none of the volunteers would have let us in today,' said Maria.

Hannah took a seat next to her. 'Which makes me think that Machi must have a guard protecting that case.'

'Why would she have someone protecting it?' asked Seb.

It was a good question, thought Hannah. Why would Machi have someone protecting it? Because it had Jesse's DNA on it? To make sure no one found it before the rubbish was collected? Then Hannah realized.

'Maybe the guard chasing us wasn't protecting it,' she said. 'Maybe he was collecting it to destroy the evidence – but we got there first!'

'I bet you're right!' said Seb.

'In that case . . .' Maria looked down at the box. 'Why am *I* still holding it?!'

'That's a good point. We need to hide it.' Hannah nodded to Seb. 'Do you think it'll fit in your backpack?'

'I can try . . .' He slung his bag on to the floor. 'Chuck it over here.'

As Maria handed it over, Hannah kept an eye on the door. There was no sign of the guard, but she didn't want to hang around here long.

Seb had managed to stuff the case into his bag and was now squeezing the zip shut. 'Done!'

Maria got to her feet. 'We need to get outta here and find Machi.'

'How do we get to the parade?' he asked.

Hannah took out her phone. 'I'll check the Official Tokyo app for updates on the parade.'

On the home page, she found a 'Parade Tracker' and looked for the most recent update. 'It's predicted to arrive at Tokyo Station in twenty minutes.'

Seb already had his phone out, searching for Tokyo Station.

'Do you think we can make it?' Hannah asked.

'It says to get on at Sendagaya Station and take the JR Sobu Line,' Seb said, 'whatever that is, and head west.'

Hannah switched to her Maps app and searched for Sendagaya Station.

'It will take us nine minutes to walk there,' Hannah said.

'You know the way?' asked Maria.

'If I follow the map, yes.' Hannah fell quiet as an older man with the Serbian flag on his shirt wandered into the refreshment room and took a seat on the sofa. He picked up the TV remote and flicked on the boxing.

Over Hannah's shoulder, Seb whispered, 'Do we know if Machi's definitely there?'

'I'm guessing so, but let's check.' Hannah switched apps again to look at Machi's most recent posts. She was in luck. Machi had uploaded a video fifteen minutes earlier beside a float with a huge anime-style red panda. The banner being carried below it was plastered with confetti.

Hannah gave Maria and Seb a nudge and showed them the video on her phone. They watched as Machi panned the camera all the way down the street.

Maria shook her head. 'Machi Mari, what are you hiding?'

The shot then flipped round to the director's face. Machi waved her microphone in the air. Hannah tapped the video with her thumb to pause it.

'Look!'

'What am I looking at?' said Maria.

'Look at what's by her feet.'

Maria brought the phone to her face. 'A white box!'

'A white case with gold detail.' Hannah nodded towards Seb. 'To replace the one she wants destroyed – the one *we* have.'

'Do you think the medal is in the one she has?' asked Seb.

'I doubt it,' Hannah decided. 'Why would she ditch one case, just to put the medal in another one?'

The Kenyans left the room to return to the prep area, leaving only the trio and the Serbian coach, who was now transfixed by the boxing.

'But it must prove that the case in my backpack is Machi's,' Seb whispered to the girls. 'It's identical to the one she's holding now and I haven't seen anyone else with one.'

'And,' Maria added, 'there might be clues in the other case to where she's hiding the medal!'

'We need to track down Machi and discover what's in the second case,' Seb said.

Hannah wandered to the doorway 'First things first, we need to get her to confess.'

'Why not find out where she hid the medal first?' asked Seb.

'Because we don't know if there's actually anything in that case. Besides, if we find the thief, we'll get the reward.'

'She's right.' Maria nodded. 'And we've gotta confront her before anyone else does!'

'True – we've got the case, but that doesn't mean the reward is ours yet,' Seb said. 'Getting her to confess is probably the quickest way.'

Hannah glanced at the prep area. 'Her guard hasn't found us yet. We've got to risk leaving here to get to the parade.'

'Hoods up?' said Seb.

Hannah nodded and pulled hers up so it almost covered her eyes.

The trio hurried through the prep room and stepped out into the foyer. Hannah bolted for the entrance. The sliding stadium doors opened to reveal an unwelcome familiar face.

'Gotcha!'

CHAPTER 26
IT'S ALIVE

Machi's guard glared down at the friends and shook his head. 'You know stealing is wrong.'

Maria grabbed Seb and Hannah by the hand and made a break for it.

'Oh no, you don't!' shouted the guard.

Maria sprinted away, pulling Hannah and Seb with her. The man, however, was hot on their heels.

'Keep running to the end!' shouted Hannah. 'Surely there's a tunnel that leads on to the track.'

Hannah's heart pounded in rhythm to the guard's feet that thundered after them. Athletes, staff and volunteers stood open-mouthed at the unfolding chaos.

A young lady in blue emerged through a door right at the end of the corridor.

Hannah pointed to the door. 'It must be through there!'

'Hold it open, please!' yelled Maria.

The lady shot to the side and held the door ajar.

The trio shot through and Hannah slammed the door shut. They heard the sound of footsteps, then a click.

'Was that the door being locked?' Hannah asked. She didn't have a good feeling about this.

'That's all right,' said Seb, spinning round. 'We can just go through the tunnel . . .'

'But we're not in a tunnel,' Hannah said, pointing.

They were in another room, completely white, with rows and rows of chairs.

'Um . . .' she murmured. 'Where are we?'

Maria moved into the centre. 'This must be the call room. It's like a waiting room before your event.'

'Where does it lead?' asked Seb.

She pointed to a second door on the opposite side. 'That'll take you to the athlete tunnel.' She walked over. 'At least, that's what it's like at all the other competitions.' She tugged on the handle and the door rattled.

Seb grimaced. 'That one locked too?'

Maria tried again. 'Yeah . . .'

Feeling slightly nauseous now, Hannah re-examined the first door. She crouched under the handle and sighed. 'There is no actual lock. It must be electric.'

'You think the guard locked us in?' Maria asked.

Hannah frowned. 'I can't see who else did.'

'But how?' asked Seb.

'I don't know,' she said. 'He must have a key or the security codes.'

Seb took a seat on a fold-up chair and reached for his drink in his rucksack. 'Wow, my throat is suddenly so dry.' He took a swig of water and grimaced. 'How long are we going to be in here for?'

'Well . . .' Maria gave the door a wallop. 'We're trapped in here until the volunteers come back for the finals. Stupid doors . . .'

Hannah sank into the corner. 'This is bad. So, so bad.' She fumbled in her pocket for her phone and asked the others, 'Should I call my dad? Or my mum? Or Ren?' She shoved her hand back in her pocket. 'Ugh, I need to stop biting my nails!'

Maria tried both doors again, shoving and rattling, but they didn't budge.

Hannah rested her chin on her fist. 'There must be some way out! For all we know that guard could be ratting us out to Machi as we speak.'

'He might not be,' Seb said. 'Don't you think she already knows we know she's the thief?'

Maria nodded. 'After all, it was probably Machi who sent that text message.'

'But how?' said Hannah. 'She won't have Seb's number.' She lowered her voice. 'If you know the right people, you can find anyone's number.'

'Well, if he isn't with Machi, he's probably still waiting for us on the other side of that door.' Hannah picked up her satchel and got to her feet. 'I'm not going to sit around waiting. There must be a way out.'

'We could use that,' Maria said.

Hannah followed her gaze over to a white plastic box on wheels. 'What for?'

Maria wandered over to the box. 'We could use it as a ramming device.'

Seb laughed. 'What even is it?'

'I don't know.' Maria craned her neck to see round the back. 'No way!'

'What?'

Maria's eyes lit up. 'I think it's a cleaning robot.' She turned to Hannah and smirked. 'We could try switching it on and turning it to maximum speed. Then angling it at the door.'

Hannah raised her eyebrows. 'Really? I guess we can try it.'

Maria searched the robot for a switch. 'This better work.'

The robot lit up in bright blue and began speaking in Japanese.

Seb shook his head. 'If it's voice-activated, we're screwed.'

'It's got buttons, but I dunno what they mean,' said Maria. 'Oh, it's alive!' The machine shot forward. 'It's got a mind of its own!'

Hannah ducked behind a chair as the machine started spurting steam. 'Maria! What did you do?'

'I don't know.' She began randomly hitting buttons, but it only let out another gush of steam and surged to the opposite side of the room. As Maria did her best to slow down the robot, Seb nudged Hannah.

'Psst, Hannah.'

'Yeah?'

'I can think of one way to get that door unlocked.' Seb pointed to the fire alarm beside the door. 'The doors would have to unlock if we set it off.'

'But it would cause chaos.'

'Yeah, but the guard is probably waiting for us outside? The chaos would hide us from him.'

Hannah looked up at the digital clock above the second door. It was 2.39 p.m. 'I guess it is the break between qualifiers and finals, so we won't be disturbing anything.'

'Exactly.'

The steaming robot began charging right towards them. Running after it, Maria waved her arms. 'This was a bad idea!'

Seb gave Hannah one last look. 'Alarm?'

She nodded. 'Alarm.'

He ran over to the door and smashed the glass cover with his water bottle. A piercing siren rang out.

'Ugh, the noise!' Hannah covered her left ear with her hand and pressed the other to her shoulder. 'Let's get out of here!'

'That's how it gets people out of the building!' Seb shouted. He tried the door handle and waved to the others. 'It's open.'

The girls rushed over to the doorway and peered into the corridor. Hannah looked around for the guard, but it was impossible to recognize anyone amongst the swarm of people.

'I can't see Machi's guard,' Hannah said. 'So, we'll run on three.' She turned to Seb and Maria. 'Ready?'

They put their hoods up and nodded.

'One . . . Two . . . Three!'

The three of them slipped into the corridor and followed the swarm of people heading towards the foyer.

Hannah could hardly see where she was going, as they were packed into the corridor like a tin of sardines – if sardines could shriek at the top of their lungs while running for cover. The trio found themselves wedged in a mishmash of people with no way of knowing how far along the corridor they were. But there was only one thing that mattered. They had to be hidden from Machi's guard. Hannah looked over her shoulder at the horde behind them. No sign of him yet. As she turned her head back she noticed somebody from the corner of her eye. Somebody tall. Somebody broad. She took another good look . . . There was no mistaking who it was.

'*Oh no!*' Hannah mouthed to the others. '*He's here!*'

Seb peered from under his hood. 'Just keep moving and stay quiet.'

Maria grabbed each of their hands. 'When I say go, we duck down and weave around people. We'll get out faster that way.'

As the procession of people rounded the corner Maria yelled, 'Let's go!'

It seemed Maria was an expert at ducking and diving through crowds. Minutes later, they were squeezing through the automatic doors at the athletes' entrance and running up the bus slope. When Hannah swung around, the guard was nowhere in sight. She took the chance to pull out a map from her notebook and showed it to Maria and Seb.

'This is where we need to go.' Hannah pointed to a spot on the map and checked behind them again. There was no sign of the guard, but that didn't mean he wasn't coming. 'Let's go!'

They began sprinting along the pavement, Maria soon pulling out in front. Still running, she twisted her head to talk to Hannah and Seb. 'When we get there, I'll tap the barriers with my family pass and we can all run through.'

They were just approaching the main road when a voice boomed behind them, 'What did I tell you about stealing?'

Hannah felt a lump in her throat as she turned her head.

'Machi's guard!' squeaked Seb.

'Run!'

CHAPTER 27
A REASONABLE EXCUSE

As the trio made it out of the Sportpark, Hannah could make out the subway station, maybe about three hundred metres away. 'It's straight ahead!' She tried to catch her breath. 'Over the road!'

'The crossing is on green!' yelled Seb.

But the timer on the traffic light was ticking down. 'There are only five seconds left! Quick!'

They darted across with a second to spare. With her heart racing and her mind whirling, Hannah looked round to see the security guard stuck on the other side, blocked by the rushing traffic.

'Hurry! So he loses sight of us!'

Maria carved a path through a sea of people on the pavement. 'Coming through! Oops, sorry, lady!' She led Hannah and Seb down a set of stairs and into

Sendagaya Station. She whipped out her family ticket at the barriers and tapped each of them through, like a military operation. 'Let's move, move, move!'

The three of them ran down another flight of stairs and followed the markings on the floor for the JR Sobu Line. They wound up on a jam-packed platform, full of people in Games merchandise.

Hannah looked up at the board. It flashed something in Japanese. She hovered for a second as it rolled over and read, NEXT TRAIN: 2 MINS.

'Two minutes?' Hannah slipped past the bustle. 'Machi's guard will have caught up with us by then.'

'So, what do we do?' asked Seb anxiously.

'Move as far down the platform as we can.'

Hannah pushed her way to the very end, just as the train arrived. Seb and Maria were close behind.

'He's here!' yelled Maria, looking over her shoulder.

Hannah saw the guard's face weaving amongst the fellow passengers. They locked eyes and the man snarled. She stepped on to the train and hauled her friends on board. The conductor blew his whistle and shouted down the platform. 'Shuppatsu Shinko! All aboard!'

The guard ducked into the nearest carriage and the train doors slid shut. Through the internal door, Hannah watched him as he ran to the adjoining carriage door and stared at them through the glass.

'Can he get in?' asked Seb.

Hannah watched as he gave the connecting door a shove. 'Doesn't look like it. We're safe for now.'

The train pulled out of the station and Maria grabbed hold of the railings. She peered up at the map on the wall. 'We're gonna have to get off at the next stop, otherwise he'll move into our carriage.'

Seb leaned in closer. 'Which stop's that?'

Hannah studied the map. 'Shinanomachi.'

'Huh!' Seb rolled his eyes. 'That's apt!'

'What's the one after that?' said Hannah.

'Yotsuya.'

Seb shrugged. 'How about we get off, then run to Yotsuya, then get back on a train into Tokyo Station? We might lose him that way.'

Maria nodded. 'It's worth a try.'

Hannah checked her phone for the time and saw there was a Tokyo Games Social app notification from ten minutes earlier. *PARADE LIVE STREAM: WATCH IT NOW!* She clicked on the video and kept an eye out for Machi's location. Hannah turned up the commentary volume to listen for any clues.

'Shh.' A man glared in her direction, pointing to a sign that read PHONES SILENT.

'Sorry,' Hannah whispered, muting the video. She clicked on the subtitles and read along.

'"... *not to forget that this will end up at one of the most famous landmarks Japan has to offer."*

"And what would that be?"

"The Shibuya Crossing, of course!"

"Of course!"'

Of course, the parade ended at the Shibuya Crossing. Hannah felt her stomach lurch. 'We're going the wrong way!'

Maria frowned. 'How come? You said that the parade was in the city centre.'

'The updates must have been slow! The live stream just said that it's on its way to the Shibuya Crossing.'

'Where's that?'

'Definitely NOT in the city centre.' Hannah flicked to Google Maps and groaned when she realized that the Shibuya Crossing was within walking distance of the stadium, but much further from Shinanomachi, the next stop. 'It'll take us ages to get there on foot.'

'But what about on a scooter?' Seb said.

Maria pushed up her glasses. 'Scooter?'

He pulled out his phone. 'There's an app on my phone so you can hire scooters. Dad said I can't use it, as kids aren't meant to. But, I think being chased by a threatening guy, after receiving threatening messages, is a reasonable excuse?'

Hannah immediately nodded. 'Let's do it.' She turned to Maria, who was already making her way to the train doors.

Maria smiled. 'I've always wanted to ride one of these. I'm in!'

As the train pulled into Shinanomachi Station, Hannah tried not to worry about everything at stake. Not catching Machi. Being caught by the guard. Even getting into trouble for riding on e-scooters. She and Seb joined Maria by the doors and waited anxiously.

'When we get out of the station,' Seb said, 'the app says there's a scooter pick-up area just to the left.'

The doors slid open and Hannah was the first to go, leaping off the train. She led the way down the heaving platform and up the stairs. She glanced back to see Maria storming up the stairs two at a time.

She heard Seb shout, 'He's on our tail!'

Hannah reached the top step and saw Machi's guard

pushing people out of his way. In the midst of the crowd, she saw a man in a pinstripe suit, just like the one Onishi had been wearing earlier. Surely Machi didn't have an Onishi Shig impersonator? What sort of tricks was she up to?

Maria ran ahead and opened the barriers with her pass. Hannah and Seb shot through and headed towards the exit. The three of them emerged into the broad daylight and turned left to the scooter park. Seb was already running over to a trio of bright orange scooters, getting out his phone to unlock them with the app.

The scooters soon began to ping to indicate they were ready to ride, and Maria and Hannah grabbed the first two. Hannah took hold of the left handlebar and looked at the exit of the station. The guard was just making his way through the barrier.

'We need to go now!' Hannah cried as Seb's scooter pinged.

They hopped on and zoomed down the long high street. The trio headed straight, until Maria took a sharp right and led Hannah and Seb along a long bending road, lined with trees. As Hannah rounded the corner she recognized the Meiji Jingu Gaien fountains, which she'd seen in her guidebook. The air was filled with the sound of tweeting birds and laughing children as people dipped their feet into the water, no doubt a relief from the hot summer sun. But there wasn't any time to take in the scenery, as Maria took a swift left and dashed across the road. Hannah's heart pounded in her chest as she gripped the throttle of the scooter. Her eyes darted from person to person, car to car, with the guard's image lurking in her mind. The pavement widened out and Seb scooted up alongside her.

'We've lost him! He must be miles back.'

'That doesn't mean he's gone!' Hannah dared to look back over her shoulder. The guard was

certainly out of sight, but he didn't seem to be the type that easily surrendered.

Seb laughed. 'We're travelling way faster than he is! As long as our scooters are charged and Maria still knows the way, we'll be fine!'

'But what if he knows we're heading to Machi? He'll jump on a train, make it to the parade before us and be waiting for us when we get there!'

'But what if he doesn't know?'

Hannah shook her head. 'Of course he knows! We have her case! *You* have her case!'

'All right, then,' Hannah rolled her eyes. 'What if he's on a scooter too? He could catch us up at any minute.'

Now on the new road, they began to sail under a tunnel of golden leaves. The sun shone through the gaps in the trees and lit up the path like a disco ball. Meanwhile, Hannah's head spun like one. The rush of everything as it passed and the thoughts circling her mind soon made her feel dizzy. She slowed down for a second. She saw all the colours of the park. The blue sky, the golden ginkgo trees, and the deep green grass. She took a deep breath. *Mmm, freshly cut grass.* She felt her heart rate start to settle.

Seb slowed down beside her and steadied her scooter

with his hand. 'You all right?'

'Yeah, thanks.' She turned to face him. 'Just felt a little dizzy, but I'm okay.'

'You sure?'

She nodded. 'Nothing's going to stop me from getting that case to Machi and sorting out this mystery at last.'

'Then let's get going. Where's Maria?'

Hannah turned to the pavement and squinted. It was full of pedestrians, from businesspeople to dog walkers, but not one of those pedestrians was Maria.

CHAPTER 28
NEVE

Hannah and Seb got off their scooters. It was too busy here to ride, and they had no idea which way Maria had gone anyway. Hannah got up on to her tiptoes to look through the sea of people on Meiji Jingu Gaien Avenue. Where was their friend?

'How are we going to find her?' She sighed.

'It's only going to get busier,' said Seb. 'The finals are soon.'

'If we don't get past the crowd, Machi's guard is going to catch us!' Hannah's stomach dropped. 'What if he finds Maria? She's all on her own!'

'What should we do?'

'If only Maria had a phone!' Hannah sighed. 'We'll have to ask someone if they've seen her.' She spotted a group of British tourists with varying levels of sunburn and Team GB caps on their heads.

The two of them managed to push their scooters through to the group and pulled them to one side.

'Hi, excuse me!' said Seb. 'Have you seen a girl on a scooter? She's got brown hair, wearing glasses?'

'Oh yes!' An older lady nodded.

'Amazing!' said Hannah. 'Where did you see her?'

The lady pointed to the end of the road. 'Up there. Heading east . . . or is it west? Oh, I never know!' She brought her finger to her lips. 'Let's just say she went right.'

Hannah and Seb gave each other a look. Not the most helpful answer . . .

They thanked the lady and turned right anyway, but there was still no sign of Maria. They carried on until they were faced with yet another crossroads.

'Left, right or straight ahead?' asked Hannah.

Seb studied the map on his phone. 'The crossing is south-west from here . . . so maybe she went straight on?'

'Are you sure?'

'I don't know!' He looked around, shrugging. 'You want to ask someone else?'

'That's going to take for ever! Each time we stop, we fall further behind.'

'It's better than going in the wrong direction.'

Seb jumped in front of an unsuspecting local girl. 'Excuse me!'

'Ah!' She stepped back.

'Have you seen a girl on a scooter? She has brown hair and wears glasses,' he asked again.

She frowned. 'Huh?'

Hannah recognized the same confusion that had been on the faces of the volunteers in the food hall. 'Maybe she doesn't speak English?'

Seb pointed to the scooter and then Hannah and himself, before holding up a finger to indicate one more. 'You see?' He put his hands to his forehead and mimed searching for something.

'Ah!' The woman pointed to the path on the right. '*Sochira-gawa*!'

Sochira-gawa?

Seb bowed in thanks and set off.

Hannah zoomed after Seb. 'This better be the right way!'

'The girl seemed confident.'

'Are you sure she understood you?'

'Yeah!'

They flew past a long row of houses.

Hannah panted. 'It doesn't feel like we're getting closer to the crossing. This looks more residential!'

Seb dropped back alongside her. 'You don't trust her, do you?'

'I don't know. How could she not have a clue about what you were saying and then be so sure about the answer?'

Seb shot past a family getting into their car. 'What are you saying?'

Hannah thought about the Onishi lookalike at Shinanomachi. 'Machi will know we're after her. That girl might be working for Machi.'

'You think she sent us in the wrong direction?'

'It's possible!'

They followed the second row of houses all the way up to a main road and past a high school, a pet store and a golf academy.

There was no sign of Maria anywhere.

'Can you see her?' asked Seb.

'This clearly isn't right!' Hannah growled. 'Which way do you want to go?'

'I don't know,' said Seb, shrugging. 'Where even are we?'

She looked to her right. 'Well, that road looks like it takes us back to where we came from.'

'So do you want to go left?'

Hannah tried to read the road sign on the other side of the crossing. 'Can you see what that says?'

'What what says?'

'The street sign on the traffic light.'

'The one above the girl in white?'

The girl in white. An American tracksuit.

'Wait!' Hannah squinted at the girl on the other side of the crossing. 'That's Maria!'

They shot over the crossing, to a black-and-white-striped building. Hannah could see Maria's bright orange scooter.

'Maria!' shouted Seb.

Maria had been frowning at a teenager's tourist map, but looked up. 'You found me!' She dropped the scooter and gave them both a hug. 'It's a good job you did because Leo's map is confusing!' She turned to the teenager beside her. 'Sorry.'

'It's okay.' He chuckled. 'It was nice to meet you, even if my map couldn't help.'

Maria crouched down and fussed the boy's big white dog on his lead. 'Bye-bye, Neve!'

Neve shuffled away

from the trio and barked.

'*Ehi!*' Leo pulled on her lead. '*Tranquilo!*'

She kept barking in Maria's direction.

'What is it?' Maria asked, stroking the dog some more.

They all glanced down the street and found out. Machi's monster was storming down the pavement towards them. Hannah noticed a slight limp in his step while he weaved around pedestrians. She placed one foot on her scooter and turned to Maria.

'Know the way to the Shibuya Crossing?'

Maria switched her scooter back on. 'Not from here.'

'I do!' Leo told the trio. 'Keep heading south-west until you get to Aoyama-dori Avenue. Then follow the road and it will take you to the crossing.'

'Awesome, thanks, Leo! You're a legend!' Maria turned to the others. 'Sorry for losing you. Let's go get Machi!'

As they set off, Leo called out behind them, 'When the road splits, remember to stay on the right-hand side!'

Maria took off first and the other two followed.

'Do you know where you're going?' Hannah called out behind her.

'I remember some of the street names on Leo's map,' she yelled back. 'Dunno for sure, but I think I do.'

They raced down the little side streets in the direction

of Aoyama-dori Avenue. Each time they came to a turn, crossing or junction, Maria shouted out the direction and Hannah and Seb scooted after her. The further they went, the narrower the roads and the busier the pavements became.

After the series of narrow streets, Maria pulled into an even smaller alleyway full of shrubs and trees.

'You sure this is right?' asked Hannah. She batted a branch out of her way. 'This doesn't *feel* right.' As she ducked under the leaves, she saw the rest of the path. Little cafe chairs were squashed on either side and straight ahead of them there was a huge glass building.

'What is that?' said Seb.

Hannah focused on the pavement and tried not to swerve into any cafe customers.

'I think it's a shopping mall! I remember seeing it on the map,' replied Maria. 'We're not going in it, are we?'

'I don't see a way around it!'

Maria rode inside and Hannah nervously did the same. There were food shops everywhere, from patisseries to noodle bars. 'If we keep going straight, the main road to the crossing should be on the other side!' Maria called over her shoulder.

Hannah saw a bright light from the other side of the

food court. She picked up the pace and raced to the other side. As the three of them neared the exit, she heard the beeping of car horns. 'Did you hear that?' she yelled. 'We must be near a busy bit!' She breathed a sigh of relief. 'Maria, I think you're right! How did you remember all of that?'

'I don't know,' Maria said, 'I just do!'

They shot out of the food court and out on to the pavement.

Seb looked around. 'Which way do we go from here?'

Maria pointed her scooter to the right. 'If this is Aoyama-dori Avenue, the Shibuya Crossing is straight down there.'

The trio set their scooters to maximum speed and hurtled along the pavement. With Maria at the front carving their path, Hannah and Seb tucked in behind her. They shot past a university, an artisan farmers market, and what seemed like millions of tall cream office blocks. Finally they reached an enormous junction, with cars coming from every which way.

Hannah called out to Maria. 'Remember what Leo told us?'

'That the crossing is on this road?'

Hannah pointed to the road veering off to the right.

'He told us to stay right.'

'But that's a new road.' Maria pointed to the road sign above them. 'Miyamasu-Zaka.'

Hannah's heart raced faster. 'Well, what do you want to do?'

'I say we go down the new road.' The girls turned to Seb and he shrugged. 'If Leo said keep right, then I think we should stay on this side of the pavement.'

'I guess there's only one place we can go,' said Maria.

They veered right and set out on what they hoped would be the last leg of the journey. With the heat bearing down on the city, Hannah felt sweat trickling down her forehead. Please could the crossing just appear!

'We made it!' Maria suddenly yelled, stopping under a railway bridge.

Hannah pulled up alongside her and caught her first glimpse of the parade.

Through the bridge, she saw a row of flags, banners and smiling faces. Towering over it all were electric billboards displaying brightly coloured cartoon-character adverts. Hannah heard a fanfare in the distance, followed by a huge cheer.

'It sounds like the parade is coming from the left,' said Seb. 'We should find a place a little further down and catch Machi by surprise.'

They parked the scooters in a row of bikes, Seb quickly using the app to end their journeys, and walked up to the crowd.

'Ready?' asked Seb.

Hannah took one final look over her shoulder. The only people she could see running towards them were people on their afternoon jog. The coast was clear for now. It was time to get Machi to confess.

Hannah sighed. 'All this investigating, all this sneaking around; it all comes down to this.'

'Aren't you excited?' Seb said, wide-eyed.

'Yeah . . . It's just . . . What if it goes wrong?'

Maria shook her head. 'You're thinking about this the wrong way! What if it goes right?'

CHAPTER 29
ONE OF A KIND

Hannah, Maria and Seb did their best to squeeze their way through the gaps in the crowd. They were almost at the front when a muffled speaker mounted in the street announced the arrival of the first float. Hannah sprang as high as she could. 'I can see it!' she cried. 'We're right on time!'

The man in front covered his ears from her shrieking and moved out of her way.

Maria winked at her friends. 'It's here! It's here! It's really here! I can't believe it!'

Their excessive shrieking drove the nearby people out the way and the friends pushed forward. Maria smiled at the others. 'Moral of the story: being loud gets you what you want.'

Hannah tried to force her way past a cluster of

teenagers in front of her. 'But we're still not close enough! Machi will be here any minute and we *cannot* miss her!'

Hannah felt a tap on her shoulder. She turned to see a gaggle of tourists pointing cameras in their direction.

'Can we have a photo of you three with the float?' one asked.

'Uh . . .' She looked at the American flag on her sleeve. Of course, she realized, they still looked like athletes! She gave the man a sheepish smile. 'Yeah . . . Sure . . .'

The music from the parade was now ringing out across the street, as Seb and Maria shuffled closer into the shot. Hannah stretched her neck to see a black convertible only five buildings away. It had to be the film crew. She had an idea and whispered to the others.

'We need to pretend that we're in the parade.'

'What?' Seb said through a forced smile.

'We have to get to the front of this crowd. If we tell them that we're late for the next part of the parade, maybe they'll let us through.'

'Everybody look this way!' The man waved from behind his camera.

'Uh . . . actually.' Seb put on his American accent and pointed down the street. 'We're in the next bit of the parade. We need to go.'

The man lowered his camera. 'Do you at least have time for one?'

Hannah could now see Machi filming out of the back of the convertible, moving ever closer towards them. 'Sorry, maybe later.' She turned to the crowd and spotted half a gap to force her way through. 'Quick!' she ordered the others. 'Through there!'

Hannah lunged into the space and Seb yelled out, 'Excuse me, coming through! We're part of the parade!'

The people

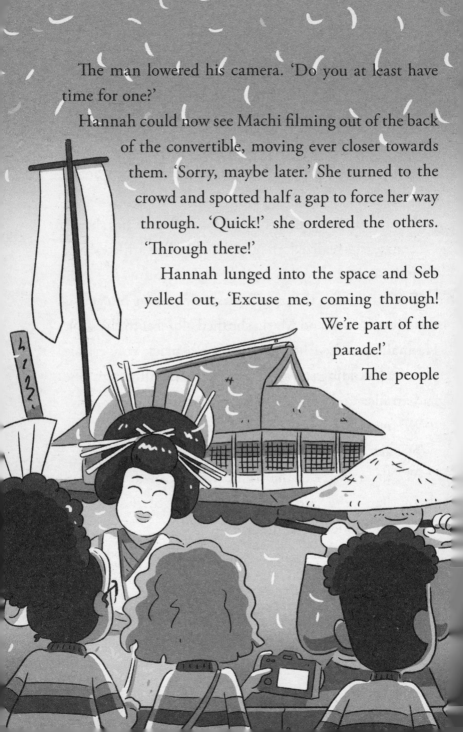

at the front of the crowd all turned round and tried to clear out of their way.

As Hannah neared the front, she caught another glimpse of the approaching car. Inside was another woman sat next to Machi. She was small and dainty, and more importantly, she was clutching the other white-and-gold case. She must be another assistant.

'I can see the case!' Hannah hissed.

'How far away is it?' asked Maria, making her way out of the huddle.

Hannah pulled herself up to the barrier and shot a glance down the street. 'About thirty seconds.'

Everyone around them erupted into cheers and began to take photos of the spectacular arrival. Dancers swirled around in flowing skirts, while a brass band marched in unison. Then the billboards lit up in what seemed like every different colour, and shop owners threw pink confetti from their windows. The first float was a crimson model Minka, an intricate replica of an ancient Japanese house. Hannah half-heartedly waved to the performers in their pristine white-and-gold kimonos. *Sorry for what's about to happen*, she thought. Machi was a matter of metres from the friends, and Hannah felt all of her muscles tense up.

'We need to stop Machi's car now!' she said.

'How are we going to do that?' shouted Maria.

Hannah scoured the pavement for something to throw, but all that was on offer was harmless confetti. She leaned over the barrier. 'We need something to get in the way.'

As Machi's car drew level with them, Seb darted further up the pavement.

'Where's he going?' Hannah cried.

Seb poked out from amongst the crowd.

'Seb!' yelled Maria.

He forced a section of the barrier out the way and

broke out on to the street. Seb ran into the middle of the road, waving his arms at the driver.

'No!' Hannah cried, and the girls stormed after him.

'Seb, move!' yelled Hannah.

But Seb didn't move. Instead, Hannah saw him bracing himself as the driver braked and Machi's camera went flying into the windscreen. The car stopped centimetres from Seb's toes and Hannah dropped to her knees in relief.

'What on earth was that?!' Machi shrieked.

A police officer came running over and the driver explained, 'We almost hit an athlete. He came out of nowhere!'

Machi turned to Seb and spat, 'You broke my camera!' She ordered her assistant to sort out the mess.

'Seb, what were you thinking?' shouted Hannah. She got up and gave him a hug. 'I'm so glad you're okay, but you're a fool!'

'I stopped the car!' He chuckled.

Maria rolled her eyes. 'Your life is worth more than a sixty-thousand-dollar reward!'

The policewoman signalled for back-up. 'Hey, you three. You may be athletes, but you can't stop the parade!' She grabbed Seb by the hand. 'What were you doing?'

'Wait!' he protested. 'We're not really athletes – we've been in disguise trying to find out who stole Jesse Marks's medal, and we think we know who it is!'

Her fellow officers arrived and took hold of Hannah and Maria. The policewoman turned to Seb. 'You think you know who the thief is?'

'Yes!'

'How do you know?'

Seb reached for his pocket. 'We've been trying to find it and I received a threat telling me to stop,' he replied calmly. 'Maybe you can trace who the message is from to prove it's them?'

'So you don't actually know who stole the medal?'

'Yes, we do. We have case notes too!' Seb gestured to Hannah. 'She can show you everything we know.'

The officers nodded to each other.

'Slowly,' the woman said.

Seb placed his phone in her hand, with the threatening message showing, and Hannah passed her notebook to the policeman guarding her.

The policewoman let go of Seb. 'Okay, then, where do you think the medal is?'

Seb turned to Machi, who was now ordering the band to keep playing. 'Dancers!' she screamed. 'Don't stop!'

But the band fell silent and everything suddenly felt eerily quiet.

Seb whispered to the officer, 'Machi Mari has it.'

The policewoman asked Machi and her assistant to step out of the car.

The director slammed the door shut and glared at the friends. 'What's all this fuss? You're ruining my film!'

The policewoman walked over. 'These three have a suspicion that you're in possession of Jesse Marks's gold medal.'

'They are obviously wrong! Why do you listen to them?'

The street was silent as the officer shook her head.

'Sorry, but no. If someone makes a claim, we investigate it.' She glanced at Seb. 'Even if it is odd.'

'It's the truth!' he insisted. 'Isn't it, Hannah? Check her white case!'

Hannah gave a sheepish grin. They had worked it all out. Yet, they didn't have any actual proof. Hannah bit her nails as she had a sudden thought: What if Machi hadn't actually stolen Jesse's medal?

The police officer held out her arm to Machi. 'May I look inside your case, please?'

Machi's young assistant began to hand it over, but Machi snatched it from her grasp.

'How dare you!'

Hannah smiled. Maybe they were right to be suspicious of Machi after all?

'Please, Ms Mari,' asked another officer, 'so we can get this parade back underway.'

She let go of the case and the policewoman balanced it on the car bonnet. She undid the clasps and lifted the lid. Hannah tried to sneak a peek of the contents, but a stern glare from the policeman behind her told her to think again. She stepped back and waited.

'No medal here.' The policewoman waved her hand. 'You shouldn't be wasting our time like this.'

Hannah's stomach plummeted. It was over just like that. She closed her eyes and hoped that everything would disappear. Not only had they failed, but she'd humiliated herself in front of hundreds of people. They'd been too hasty.

'Wait!' Maria blurted. She lowered her voice and smiled. 'Did you check all the compartments?'

Of course, thought Hannah. That was why they were a good team – they each had their own qualities and completed different pieces of the puzzle.

The policewoman sighed and did a thorough search of the case. She lifted a small flap at the bottom and her eyes widened. As she put on a pair of gloves, Hannah's heart seemed to be trying to escape from her chest.

Before the police officer could utter the words herself, Hannah grinned. 'You've found it!'

The woman lifted the gleaming medal from the case and held it by the ribbon. 'It appears that we have.'

The crowds all around them gasped.

'That's impossible!' Machi ran over to the case. 'I never touched the medal!'

The policewoman gave it to one of her colleagues, who bagged it for evidence. 'Now, Ms Mari,' she said, 'please calm down. You are under arrest for the theft of Jesse Marks's medal.'

'Calm down?!' Machi stamped her foot. 'I'm being framed! Test it! You'll find not one of my fingerprints is on that medal!' She lunged for the case, but the policewoman pulled her back. 'I don't know how it got in there!' She stared at the case. 'Wait – you must check the engraving.'

'What engraving?' the policewoman asked.

'My name is under the handle,' Machi barked.

The woman's colleague lifted the handle and frowned. 'Nothing on this one I'm afraid.'

'That proves it!' Machi beamed. 'My case is engraved with my name. That case cannot be mine.' She wagged her finger at her assistant. 'Lisa, did you take my case and replace it with this one?'

'No!'

'Where is my case?!' Machi demanded.

Seb swung his backpack on to the floor. 'I might have it . . .' He tugged out the white case and lifted the handle.

She paced over and snapped, 'What's that?'

'We found it in the store-room.' He held the case to his chest. 'Uh, if your name was on it, what would it look like?'

'It says *Machi Mari* in Art Deco writing.' She flourished her wrist. 'You know, with diamonds on either side.'

Seb turned the case around. There was some Japanese writing engraved on a tiny Gatsby-style gold plate. 'I don't know what it says . . .'

The policewoman walked over and examined it. 'I can confirm that is Machi's name.'

'So this proves I'm not the thief!' Machi bellowed. 'Someone tried to frame me!'

'I don't know.' The policewoman took Machi's actual case and set it down on the floor. 'Ms Mari, are both of these yours?'

'No! I only have one white-and-gold case! It's limited edition. I bought it last week.'

Hannah's brain was whirring. Everything was getting more complicated by the second. If Machi only had one bag, then one of them must have been planted by someone else.

'For the record,' said the police officer, 'can you officially identify which one is yours?'

Machi pointed to the case on the ground. 'This is mine! As they're one of a kind, they're all numbered, and you can see that mine is number one.'

The policewoman nodded. 'Thank you.' She turned to a younger colleague over by the car and said something in Japanese, then swung back around to address Seb, Hannah and Maria. 'He is going to check the number on the other case, then go to the shop and find out who purchased it. But you three have to explain yourselves.'

Hannah panicked. With this plot twist, she had no idea who the real thief was. It didn't seem to be Machi?

Unless she was an even better actor than Seb?

'This is going to sound a little crazy . . .' started Hannah.

The officer chuckled. 'All of this is crazy!'

Hannah smiled nervously as her brain tried to slot the puzzle pieces into place. 'Okay . . . so I was initially suspicious of Machi, after we found her perfectly new case in the bin. Then, just now, when Machi said that she only has the first of a few limited-edition cases, she seemed genuine – and it doesn't surprise me that Machi wants everything about her life to be "number one". It figures she'd have the first limited-edition case.'

Several of the police officers nodded.

'This makes me think . . .' said Hannah. 'How does Machi end up with a case that isn't hers? She wouldn't pick one up accidentally, would she? So it must have been planted.'

The policewoman held up her hand. 'That is a big assumption.'

'But it's possible! My friends and I spoke to a Games volunteer called Sakura, and she said that Machi has a new assistant almost every day.'

'That's because they're always trying to find out my secrets!' Machi frowned. 'I can't trust anyone! They leak horrible stories about me to the press, when all I want to do is work on my projects.'

Machi seemed truly upset by this, and Hannah felt a little sorry for her.

'Whatever the reason,' Hannah continued, 'if Machi has a new assistant each day, it's a really easy way for someone to get close to her.'

Lisa gasped. 'You think I planted the case?'

'No.' Hannah thought back to Machi's other assistant. 'You had a tall red-headed assistant yesterday, didn't you?' Hannah asked Machi.

'Ugh, yes. I fired her and it was only halfway through the day. I was so desperate after she left that I found Lisa on the concourse.'

Hannah thought back to yesterday. It was like the other girl hadn't even wanted to work for Machi. It was all beginning to make sense.

'I think that girl needed to get close to you.'

Machi took a seat on the bonnet of the car. 'I told you, they all do. They want my secrets!'

'This one is different, though. She didn't want secrets. She wanted to switch the cases.'

'I asked her to fetch my new lens for me yesterday and she told me the case was empty. I thought she'd stolen all my stuff – that's why I fired her!'

Hannah looked at the empty case. 'She may have done that too.'

'So she framed me and sabotaged my documentary? Who would do that?'

'I think I know . . .' Hannah turned to Maria and Seb. 'You remember who we saw her with, don't you?'

Seb looked around. 'Other than Machi?'

Maria's eyes suddenly boggled behind her glasses, and Hannah guessed she'd realized.

'Her name is Cari,' Hannah explained. 'She's been working for someone else all week.'

The policewoman stepped forward. 'Who?'

Hannah took a deep breath. 'She works for Onishi Shig.'

CHAPTER 30
NO CHANGES

The parade had been stopped all this time, but the crowd didn't seem to mind – there was a new spectacle on show. The people who had lined either side of the street were now gathered around Machi's car. All eyes were on Hannah as, slowly but surely, all the clues were falling into place in her mind.

'I can't believe we didn't see it earlier!' she said.

'See what?' asked Seb.

'That Onishi was involved!'

Murmurs rippled down the street.

'The guard wasn't Machi's!' Hannah explained. 'He was Onishi's.'

The policewoman quickly turned to Hannah. 'What guard?'

Hannah paused for a moment to think about exactly

how she'd say this. 'After the three of us found the case, we saw Onishi near the track. Then as soon as we left, a man started chasing us. We thought Machi had hired someone to protect or destroy the case.'

'Uh, this is not true,' Machi chimed in.

'Mmm, hmm . . .' Hannah quickly moved on. 'I believe that the guard was Onishi's. He wasn't guarding the case. He was following us.'

'What makes you think that?' the policewoman asked as she scribbled some notes down.

'Well . . .' Hannah held out her hand only to realize how much she was shaking. Her accusations had to be right otherwise they'd be in serious trouble. She moved her hand back down by her side and fought the urge to bite her nails. 'The man didn't start chasing us until after we spoke to Onishi. If he'd been guarding the case, then he would have been after us as soon as we left the storeroom.'

'Storeroom?' The policewoman raised her eyebrow.

'Uh, yes.' Hannah's eyes darted from the woman to her flipbook. This was the part of the explanation she wasn't looking forward to. They'd snuck into the athletes' section and set off the fire alarm, after all. Would they be in trouble for that?

'Wait!' Seb turned to Hannah. 'You know the threats I received? Do you think the guard sent them?'

She flashed him a smile. 'That's a good question!' Hannah said, relieved Seb had changed the subject. 'But, no, I don't, because I've worked out who did.'

The policewoman nodded. 'Okay, then.'

'Thanks.' Hannah gave a half-smile as she thought back to all her meticulous notes in her notebook. 'So . . . Seb received the text after we'd met Onishi's son, Ren. Seb gave Ren his number and we called him later that day. He guessed that we were trying to find the medal thief. Seb, can you show the threats?'

Seb unlocked the phone for the officers and they read the messages. Meanwhile, Hannah continued, 'My guess is that Onishi overheard a phone call between Ren and Seb, and realized what we were doing. He must have found Seb's number in Ren's phone and sent him the threat from a private number.'

The policewoman took Hannah's notebook from the male officer and flipped through the pages. 'You have a long story, but do you have any evidence?' She passed the book back.

The three friends looked at one another. Apart from the threatening texts, they had nothing. Even if Hannah *could* prove that Onishi had sent them, she couldn't prove that it had anything to do with the medal.

Hannah felt like she'd been punched. It wasn't enough. She'd worked it out, but there was no proof. Onishi had been clever. Hannah turned to the policewoman and sighed. 'I'm afraid not.'

'Then I will have to call your parents and take you to the police station to question you more.' She turned to her fellow officers. 'You can escort these—'

She was cut off by the roar of a police car coming up the street. It passed all the floats and parked up by the side of the road. The crowd eagerly watched as the driver stepped out and closed the door. Hannah recognized him instantly. It was the officer who had gone to check who had purchased the planted case. He walked over to the policewoman and pulled out a thin slip of paper, handing it to her.

Hannah tried to make out the writing from the other side, but the letters were too tiny.

'This,' the officer said, addressing the trio as well as the policewoman, 'is a signed receipt for case number twelve, which was purchased yesterday morning. The product is so expensive that the shop asks for its customers' signatures when they buy.'

'It must also show the account that paid for it,' the policewoman said. 'We can trace this back to its owner.'

'We don't have to,' the younger officer said, pointing to the top of the receipt. 'The customer's name is at the top and their signature is here.

'So . . .' Machi came closer. 'Whose case is it?'

'Mr Shig's.'

'Shoot, it *was* him!' Maria gasped.

'He didn't use a fake signature!' said Hannah. 'Rookie mistake.'

'But . . .' Seb frowned. 'Onishi was so nice! How could he do something like that?'

Machi waved her arms. 'Jealousy.'

Hannah turned to the male officer holding her notebook. 'Um, excuse me?'

'Yes?'

She pointed to his hand. 'Could I take a look at that, please?'

He looked around. 'You can read it, but no changes. That would be tampering with evidence.'

'Thank you.' She flicked to her notes about their chat with Ren at the stadium. 'I'm just checking something . . .'

In the meantime Machi was talking to the ever-increasing number of photographers and film crew.

'Onishi is threatened by my career and wants to end it.' She tossed her hair back and laughed. 'He thought he could take me down with a scandal!'

Hannah finally found the point she was looking for: *New directors stealing old directors' jobs.*

'Of course!' she cried.

Everyone turned to Hannah.

'What?' asked Machi.

She laughed nervously. 'I can't believe I'm saying this, but Machi is right.'

'See, I am innocent!'

'Ren complained that the new directors were taking over, and . . .' Hannah flipped a couple of pages further. 'Maria also saw lots of articles about Onishi, saying that it was time for him to go.'

'It's true, I did!' Maria nodded.

'A failing career is bad enough, but there was something bigger at stake.' Hannah looked up at the policewoman. 'Sakura told us that Machi was likely to be made the official documentary-maker for the Emperor of Japan. No doubt Onishi wanted that job too, and needed a way of making sure that his younger rival didn't get it.'

The cameras snapped away and Hannah shielded her eyes from the flashes. 'The only thing that I can't work out . . . is how Onishi stole the medal . . .'

Seb came over to take a look at the book. 'What do your notes say?'

The male officer held out his arm. 'No changes.'

'Don't worry.' Seb took a step back. 'No changes.' He held his hands behind his back and leaned over the pages. 'Surely there must be something in there. You wrote down everything!'

Hannah shook her head. 'I know who did it, why he did it and how he made it look like someone else did it. But I can't figure out how!'

'Maybe someone did it for him,' said Maria 'You know, like that guard.'

The guard. The guard, the guard, the guard!

Hannah snapped her notebook shut. 'Maria, you're right! That man chasing us was more than Onishi's guard. We've seen him before.'

'You mean at the stadium?'

'No!' She pictured the top knot on his head. 'He was in the athletes' village! At the bus stop! He was operating the security scanners!'

The policewoman looked up from her notes. 'Can you clarify what you mean?'

Hannah nodded. 'I think the guard took the medal out of

Jesse's pocket when he entered the village. Jesse would have put his jacket in the tray when he went through security, and with it his medal. The medal went into the scanner, but never came out, because Onishi's guard took it.'

The policewoman brought her pen to her lips. 'It is interesting that you say this. During our investigation, we found that the security cameras were turned off at the exact time of Jesse Marks's arrival at the village.'

'No way!' Seb turned to Hannah. 'You just solved the last piece of the puzzle!'

Hannah looked around at the road, now packed with parade-goers, the press fighting their way to the front.

She beamed at Seb and Maria. 'We did it together,' she said, and they grinned back at her.

The policewoman shouted to her team, and her colleagues ran into a huddle before she spun round to address the press.

'What did she say?' whispered Maria.

'I have no idea!' Hannah laughed.

Whatever the policewoman had said, the members of the press were now forming an orderly row as they angled their cameras at the trio.

The police officer came up behind them and smiled. 'Thank you.'

Hannah turned round and returned the grin. 'I'm glad we could help.'

'Now . . .' She nodded to the ever-growing line of photographers and news crews and winked. 'Enjoy your moment.'

Hannah looked over her shoulder to see Machi was waving them over.

'I was wrongly accused of a terrible crime, and these three children cleared my name!' She turned to the people on the street and they erupted with cheers and applause.

'Over here!' yelled a voice in the press. The friends waved to the cameras and grinned.

'We did it!' Hannah squeaked. 'We solved our first case!'

Maria hopped up and down. 'Jesse's going to be so happy!'

'And I get Buster!' said Seb.

Maria nudged her glasses to the bridge of her nose. 'Who?'

Hannah laughed. 'Seb's dog, remember?'

'Oh yeah!' Maria rolled her eyes. 'How could I forget!'

'Speaking of forgetting . . .' Seb gave Hannah a nudge. 'We should probably give the accreditation and kit back. Hopefully no one will mind that we borrowed it now that Jesse will get his medal back.'

'Hold on...' Hannah saw an American flag being draped out of a shop window. 'Do these people know we're not athletes?'

Seb turned to Maria. 'Well, one of us is!'

There was a commotion further along the street, where one of the police officers had started running.

'Onishi and the guard?' Hannah yelled, recognizing their familiar outlines. 'They're here!'

Hannah saw Onishi's head poking out above the crowd. 'It *was* him following us!'

CHAPTER 31
THREE GENIUSES

The rest of the police set off down the pavement, clutching their walkie-talkies. Hannah, Maria and Seb followed in hot pursuit, ignoring the shouts of the press. They could see Onishi escaping the parade, pushing his way through people, as a pattern of shrieks rose up from the crowd. The officers shouted to each other in Japanese and darted down all the different side streets. *They must be trying to corner him*, thought Hannah. The friends followed Onishi down Koen-dori street.

Hannah saw him weaving around shoppers. 'By the sunglasses store!'

Maria bolted after him, but even she wasn't fast enough in the crowd. 'He's getting away!'

The guard managed to fight off three officers at once, and Onishi made a break for it at the traffic lights. The green man turned to red and Maria groaned. 'No, no, no!' The traffic began zooming along the road, blocking their path. 'We need to get to that side!'

Through the moving cars, Hannah spotted a ball of fluff walking towards Onishi in the opposite direction. 'Is that . . . ?' She recognized the dog's owner more than the animal itself. 'Leo!'

'Hey, Leo!' Maria yelled, jumping up and down.

He waved. 'Ah, hello!'

Maria waved her arms hysterically. 'Please stop that man!'

Leo looked down as Onishi ran towards him. Neve snarled and pulled at her lead. Leo crouched down to unclip it and Neve let out a bark, bolting down the pavement. Onishi turned to get away from the dog by crossing the road, but a parked van kept him trapped. Back at the crossing, the cars finally came to a halt again and the trio shot across.

'Corner him!' Seb yelled, and they spread out to block Onishi's path.

Onishi spun round, his eyes wide as the three of them ran towards him. His gaze darted around as he looked for a gap in the road to cross, but Neve was closing in.

The traffic on the busy road continued to stream past

and Onishi pleaded. 'Stop! Please!' Onishi yelped as Neve dived for the director like he was a squeaky toy and snatched his ankle, pulling him to the ground.

'You did it!' Hannah beamed. She, Maria, Seb and Leo all caught up with Neve. 'Well done!'

Leo laughed. 'Who are you talking to? Me or Neve?' he said as he grabbed Onishi and tied him to a lamp-post with his dog's lead.

'Well, both of you!' said Hannah.

Further down the road, Hannah saw the police running to the scene. The policewoman pulled out a pair of handcuffs.

'Onishi Shig...' she began, but the rest was all in Japanese. It didn't take a translator to know what Onishi was saying. In Hannah's head it went a little something like, *You are under arrest for the theft of Jesse Marks's gold medal. You have the right to remain silent...*

Onishi looked around in desperation and whimpered.

'What's going on?' asked Maria.

'He says he is innocent,' an officer told her, 'but we'll have to let the courts decide.'

'You're still arresting him, aren't you?'

'Yes. We do not let someone go because they say they are innocent. Everyone must face justice!'

'I don't know what's going on!' Onishi cried in English, looking at the three friends. 'What did you do?!' He shed a single tear. 'What did you tell them?'

Onishi kicked the ground and cursed. 'Fine! I planted it! I did it all!' More tears fell from his eyes, but this time, Hannah thought they seemed real. 'I love my job, and all these new directors are forcing me to finish. They take everything I have! My work, my crew, my ideas! The job for the emperor was a chance for me to keep doing what I love. What my son loves too!' His bottom lip trembled. 'But Machi had to ruin it all! I could not let her take what is mine! Ours! For me and

Ren. I did what I had to do . . .'

The policewoman sighed and spoke to him in Japanese as a police car pulled up. Onishi was steered inside just as Machi appeared, glaring at the director who'd tried to frame her. She made her way over to where Hannah, Maria, Seb and Leo stood, crouching down to Neve and scratching behind her ear. 'Hmm, good dog!'

'I'll move out of the way and let you all talk,' Leo said, looking down. 'Come on, Neve!'

Machi rested against the wall and smiled at Hannah, Seb and Maria. 'Look, I'm not sure you're really athletes . . . You look too young. But thank you.'

'I'm sorry we thought you were the thief,' said Seb.

'Forget it. You had to think it was me to realize I'd been framed.'

'I guess . . .' Hannah nodded. 'And, you're right. We're not athletes.'

'I didn't think so.' She chuckled. 'What do you really do?'

'I'm just a kid, really,' said Hannah.

'Never!' Machi moved closer. 'You're much more than that if you found all those clues. I can't imagine how you did it.'

'Well, we snuck around a lot,' Seb joked.

'That is my point!' Machi looked at Hannah. 'How many times could you have given up?'

'We only thought about it once – when Seb got that threat.'

'And *that* –' Machi smiled – 'is why you will never be "just a kid". You remind me of my younger self, you know.'

Hannah couldn't help but grin. Although she did wonder, *Am I that bossy?*

Machi turned to Maria. 'But, you . . . I think you are an athlete?'

Maria nodded, beaming. 'I am. I mean, I'm not professional yet, but I hope to be!'

'Maybe I will film you at the next Games?'

Maria squealed. 'You would?'

'Of course. It's the least I can do for you!'

The director turned to Seb. 'And what can I do for you? What are you into?'

His eyes lit up. 'Well, I want to be an actor.'

'Amazing! What school do you go to?'

'Prescott High School.'

Machi tilted her head. 'You're not at a performing arts school?'

'I'm at a club, but the acting schools in London are

'super expensive for me and my mum.'

'Hmmm, I have a friend in Los Angeles. He is in charge of entry at a performing arts school. Let me see what I can do – as a thank-you.'

Seb stood open-mouthed. 'I . . . I don't even know what to say!'

'That's awesome!' said Maria. 'Isn't it, Hannah?'

'Yeah!' Hannah forced a smile. It was amazing for Seb, but for her? She'd been thinking that Seb would be in the same country as her and they'd be able to meet up. But if he moved? Then both of her new friends would be in different continents.

Hannah heard a shout from further up the street. She looked up and saw a white tracksuit running towards them. As he came closer, Hannah realized who it was.

'Jesse!' Maria brought her hand to her face. 'How did he get here?!'

Machi stepped aside and reached for what Hannah presumed was a spare camera. 'Don't mind me filming!'

Hannah laughed. Even when Machi wasn't at work, she was working. Yes, she was harsh, but maybe Machi was a bit misunderstood too. It seemed to Hannah that she only ever wanted to do her best.

Jesse gestured to Machi and rolled his eyes. 'You three don't mind me filming, do you?'

'Nah.' Hannah smiled. 'She's all right.'

Jesse frowned, looking at their US jackets. 'You're not American?'

'I am,' Maria said. 'The other two, not so much. But we needed disguises to find your medal . . .'

'In that case, whatever you did was worth it.'

'We'll return everything!' Hannah promised.

'I can't believe you're here, Jesse!' Maria beamed.

Jesse grinned. 'I was at the back of the parade when word got out that you had found my medal. I had to find you to say thank you!'

'Then we should probably tell you that the police have it right now – sorry,' said Seb.

'That's all right – I'm sure they'll return it eventually! Anyway, I wanted to see you more than the medal!'

'We all watched you win the one hundred metres!' Maria squeaked. 'And you took my flag!'

Jesse's eyes widened. 'You're the girl who gave me the flag?'

She nodded.

'We had a photo, didn't we?' Jesse said.

'Yep!'

'Damn.' He chuckled. 'It's crazy to think that *you* found it.'

A permanent smile was stuck on Maria's face. 'I'm kinda a big fan . . .'

'Oh wait!' He pulled out his phone. 'You three probably want your reward.'

Maria laughed. 'I'd actually forgotten about that.'

Hannah hadn't, but she was glad Jesse had said something. She didn't want to ask for it!

'I'll give you my agent's email,' Jesse went on. 'He'll make sure you get it.' He pointed to himself. '*I'll* make sure you get it.'

'This is the best day of my life!' Maria yelped.

'Your life? Three geniuses have just found my medal!' He looked around as if seeing who was listening. 'I'm glad that you found it. You're proper fans, not attention-seekers or money-grabbers.'

'Really?' said Maria.

'Of course! So spend the prize money wisely.' Jesse jokingly wagged his finger.

Maria looked at Hannah. 'Oh that reminds me!'

Hannah laughed. 'What?'

She smiled. 'You know the reward is now sixty thousand dollars . . . so, I can give you your share back.'

Hannah shook her head. 'You don't have to do that!'

'I want to,' Maria assured her, 'and twenty thousand dollars is plenty.'

Jesse turned to Hannah. 'Did you give up your share?'

'Originally, yes,' she replied. 'I wanted Maria to have enough for all her training.'

'Training?'

Hannah smiled. 'You're probably looking at the next long-jump champion.'

'Oh really?!' Jesse looked at Maria.

'I hope so!' she said. 'I'm on the junior team.'

He smiled 'You're in good hands. I was on the junior team once.'

'Excuse me?' Hannah spun round to see Machi with her camera. 'Can I get a photo of you four?'

'Okay, then!' Jesse laughed. 'But only because you didn't actually steal my medal!'

'This will make the perfect photo!' Machi stepped back and angled her camera. 'Okay, everyone! Smile!'

CHAPTER 32
THE FINISH LINE

That Sunday the stadium was packed. The sun was setting on the final day of the competition and the track was lit up in gold, matching the confetti being thrown from the stands. Every single phone and camera was pointed at the middle of the field. Gone were the javelin cars and pole-vault mats. Instead, a podium stood, surrounded by volunteers in sky-blue jackets and blue trousers. Dressed in their own bespoke sky-blue jackets were Hannah, Maria and Seb, each with an honorary emperor's badge pinned to their collar. As the band played a symphony under the Japanese flag, Hannah began to feel a little nervous. She stared

at the pillow sitting on her arm. Carefully balanced on top of it were four gold medals, each carved with a Ryu dragon. She turned to Seb and Maria.

'How are you two so calm?'

Maria looked at the single medal on her own cushion. 'Because I'm excited!'

Seb grinned. 'This is the biggest stage I've ever performed on!'

'Exactly! Think of all the people watching!' Hannah grimaced, but at least holding the pillow meant it was impossible to bite her nails.

'But I'd be lying if I said I wasn't a little nervous,' Seb went on, looking down. 'What if I drop their flowers?'

The stadium went dark and a spotlight appeared at the end of the tunnel.

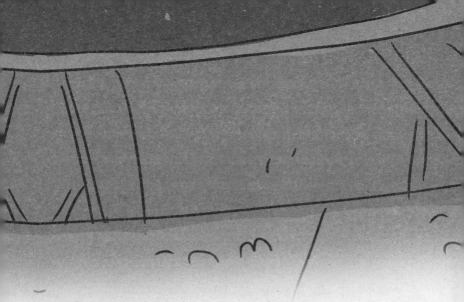

Hannah took a deep breath. 'Well, there's no going back now.'

The band began to play a fanfare and four athletes emerged on to the track.

'*Ladies and gentlemen,*' the tannoy announced, '*please welcome your gold medallists for the men's four-by-one-hundred-metre relay!*'

The fans leaped out of their seats to applaud the winning team: the USA. Their captain, Jesse, led the way over to the podium, waving to the crowd as he went. They each lined up behind the top step and awaited the signal.

The tannoy blared, '*The gold medallist and champion is the United States of America!*'

Maria jumped up and cheered. 'Whoop, whoop!'

'*The medals are awarded to: Aaron Wykoff, Marcus Draper, Ralph Lewis and Jesse Marks!*'

'That's my cue!' Hannah squeaked. She stood up straight, took a deep breath and walked to the front of the podium. Yes, she was nervous, but she also couldn't have felt prouder as she bowed to the Japanese prime minister.

'Thank you, Hannah.' He returned the bow and picked up the first medal from the cushion.

The team stepped forward and waved to the crowd. Hannah heard Maria cheer again as the prime minister hung the medal around Lance's neck. The prime minister collected the next medal and awarded it to Marcus. He bent down to receive his medal and whispered to Hannah, 'Thank you.' He kissed the medal. 'My first gold.'

She smiled and handed over the next medal for Ralph. She looked over her shoulder and grinned at Seb and Maria. They stuck up their thumbs and Hannah laughed. Who would have thought that three kids, strangers just a few days ago, would end up presenting relay champions with their gold medals? Jesse had arranged it all, and when his agent had called Hannah to tell her, she'd been speechless.

The prime minister turned to Hannah for the final relay medal.

She presented him with the cushion and he smiled. 'I think you should do the honours.' He took the cushion from her grasp. 'Here.'

Hannah picked up Jesse's medal by the ribbon. 'Woah.' She tried to keep it steady. 'These are heavy.'

Jesse bowed his head. 'That's why you wear them with your chin up and your shoulders back.'

She reached up and hung the medal around his neck. 'Thank you.' He shook her hand. 'You're a pretty awesome team leader.'

Hannah could feel herself blushing. 'That means a lot.' She turned to the crowd and gave them a cheeky wave. She knew that their applause was for the athletes, but she loved the roar. Their cheers swept the stadium and it felt as if every single hair on the back of her neck was standing up. Hannah took a deep breath and savoured the moment, before slowly returning to her place alongside the others. She smiled at Seb.

'You're up.'

He put on a big smile and walked over to the podium. As the girls watched Seb present the flowers, Hannah sighed.

'I'm going to miss this.'

Maria frowned. 'I haven't really thought about going home.'

'There are always the next Games . . .'

Maria chuckled. 'What, four years away?'

'You're right – that's rubbish.'

Maria pointed to Seb as he gave Marcus his flowers. 'We'll be spread all over the place, especially if he moves to the acting school in LA.'

'I know!'

'But maybe we'll be able to meet up. My dad's family is in America still, so we could all get together there. We could use some of our reward money!'

Hannah had already decided to give half of hers to Ren – she felt awful that he had ended up so hurt in all of this, with everything looking like his dad would go to prison. None of what Onishi had done was Ren's fault.

'Yeah!' Hannah whispered. 'We could go to a Grand Prix or the World Cup next year?'

Maria nudged up her glasses. 'Those things cost a fortune!'

'How about I just visit the next time you're in the US?'

'Sounds awesome.'

Seb returned to stand beside Hannah. 'That was epic!'

he said as the stadium continued to roar. 'I never want this week to end.'

Neither did Hannah. Yesterday they'd spent the day doing fun interviews and challenges with Jesse on his day off. They'd even made it on to a special advert for Hannah's favourite show, *Odd Squad*.

The band came to the end of their piece and a hush fell over the stadium.

The prime minister stepped forward and opened his arms to the crowd. 'And now to bring this show to a close...' He pointed to the big screen and it lit up with the words TO HANNAH, MARIA AND SEB, THE WORLD THANKS YOU!

'Amazing!' Hannah stared up at the letters. 'This could go down in history!'

The prime minister waved at Maria, and Hannah watched her walk over to join him.

'What will they write about you in the history books, Hannah?' asked Seb.

'How I took down evil geniuses and united the world. What about you?'

'Undercover stuff. Master of accents. Espionage.'

Hannah laughed. 'Can you imagine?'

They waved to Maria and the tannoy announced the

final message of the night. *'It's time to recrown your one-hundred-metre champion. Please go wild for America's very own Jesse Marks!'*

The stadium roared as Maria returned the gold medal to its rightful owner, standing on her tiptoes and looping the medal over Jesse's head.

Seb whispered to Hannah, 'It was nice of you to let her do that.'

'It was the obvious thing to do! When we present an Oscar to Tom Holland, we'll let you hand it over,' she joked.

'Naturally.' He laughed.

Hannah watched as Jesse pulled a pin badge from his pocket and pinned it to Maria's other collar.

Seb leaned over. 'Ah no way! She's got Oksana's badge and now Jesse's too!'

Jesse waved Hannah and Seb towards him. 'Over here!'

They ran over and Hannah gave Maria a huge hug. Over Maria's shoulder she saw a young girl on the other side of the stadium holding up a banner that read MY HEROES!

Jesse bent down and grinned. 'Oi, you three, come up here.'

The rest of the relay team made space for the friends

and helped them up on to the podium. They turned around to the sea of press filming and clicking to capture this perfect moment.

Seb waved to one of the cameras. 'It's Max!'

'Hi, Max!' Jesse yelled.

They all giggled and Hannah looked at their huge smiling faces on the big screen. The camera panned to the trio's family. Maria's sister bounced up and down when she saw herself, and Hannah laughed. 'She's very proud.'

Maria placed an arm on Hannah's shoulder, as Seb wrapped his arm around Hannah from the other side.

'They all are,' Maria said, 'but we should all be proud of ourselves too. We did it – we solved the Gold Medal Mystery!'

What a moment, thought Hannah. If this trip had to end, she wasn't sure it could get better than this – standing between her two new best friends as the whole world watched and cheered.

ACKNOWLEDGEMENTS

Dear Reader,

Thank you so much for reading *Thief on the Track*! It is a childhood dream come true to be an author. Nine-year-old me would be beaming over the fact that her book has made its way into your hands.

At first glance, this book is a celebration of my time at the Tokyo 2020 Paralympic Games – the excitement of travel, the roar of the crowd and the thrill of competition! But the story is also inspired by one of the greatest Olympians of all time. *Thief on the Track* began as a tribute to Jesse Owens, a hero at the 1936 Berlin Games, winning four gold medals. Jesse's story, like those of so many athletes, is one of resilience and triumph against the odds.

Which brings me to my three protagonists . . . Hannah, Seb and Maria's personalities are uniquely their own, which makes their friendship so dynamic. It is no coincidence that the emotions they feel and the lessons they learn are those that I have experienced myself, both in and out of the pool. I am so proud to bring their different experiences to life on the page. In fact, I hope that each and every reader can see themselves as they solve the mystery alongside our trio.

I have loved researching, plotting and writing this first Gold Medal Mysteries adventure and have a lot of people to thank:

My mum, the original Hannah, whose heart of gold has inspired every act of kindness and selflessness in this book.

My dad, Will, whose unsung ambition and drive has stuck with me (and now our mystery-solving trio) in everything I pursue.

My grandad, a fellow author, with whom I have developed a deep bond over our shared creativity and desire to learn.

My team, Catherine, Lucy & Lydia (to name a few), who have made writing this book the most enjoyable project – I can't wait to see what the future holds for us!

Everyone I have ever met, read about, or studied – no matter how permanent or passing. Using their stories, I have been able to delve into what makes characters who they are and defines their part in life.

Lastly, I want to thank you, my amazing reader, for choosing this book. I hope that it brings you just as much enjoyment as writing it brought me.

Happy reading!

Ellie

ELLIE ROBINSON

is a multi medal-winning British swimmer, and a world-record breaker in the 50m and 100m butterfly. She won Gold and Bronze medals at Rio 2016 and a Commonwealth Gold in 2018, before competing in the Tokyo 2020 Paralympics. Named BBC Young Sports Personality of the Year in 2016, she has also been awarded an MBE. Ellie is now a student and author, and *Thief on the Track* is her first book for children.

The race to solve the *next* exciting case is on!
Look out for

GOLD MEDAL MYSTERIES

PERIL ON THE PITCH

ELLIE ROBINSON